FIRE BELOW

"Something has happened in the station. There's been an incident involving a minisub. Some station crew were killed. We're still trying to get a handle on what's happening."

Bridger waited, letting Noyce stew.

"Admiral, what are we heading into?"

Noyce licked his lips. "That's just it, Nathan. We don't have a clue. We're getting reports from the station, and Harpe has communicated with some of his employees. But—near as we can figure it—one of the worms was brought in—"

"Alive?"

Noyce nodded. "Alive, and—we don't know—it killed someone."

seaQuest DSV

An all-new, original adventure based
on the exciting TV series!

seaQuest DSV Novels from Ace Books

seaQuest DSV

FIRE BELOW

A *seaQuest DSV* novel by Matthew J. Costello

Based on the Amblin Television
and Universal Television series *"seaQuest DSV"*
created by Rockne S. O'Bannon

ACE BOOKS, NEW YORK

seaQuest DSV: Fire Below, a novel by Matthew J. Costello, based on the Amblin Television and Universal Television series "*seaQuest DSV*" created by Rockne S. O'Bannon.

This book is an Ace original edition, and has never been previously published.

SEAQUEST DSV: FIRE BELOW

An Ace Book/published by arrangement with MCA Publishing Rights, a Division of MCA, Inc.

PRINTING HISTORY
Ace edition/January 1994

ISBN: 0-441-00039-8

ACE®
Ace Books are published by The Berkley Publishing Group, 200 Madison Avenue, New York, NY 10016.
ACE and the "A" design are trademarks belonging to Charter Communications, Inc.

PRINTED IN THE UNITED STATES OF AMERICA

10 9 8 7 6 5 4 3 2

FIRE BELOW

ONE

Whistle Stop

CHAPTER 1

The woman in the deep-ocean pressure suit reached up and quickly grabbed a metal bar dangling inches above the water.

Her name was Mary Knox. But she had dozens of names, a confused jumble of names. Here, at SousMer Underwater Resort, she was known as Mrs. Adam Ferro.

"All right," she said, her voice picked up by the EVA underwater suit's communications system and broadcast throughout the open area of this diving bay.

Her voice mixed with the gentle music being piped in, diffuse, nondescript music. Everyone staying at SousMer was familiar with the liquid, synthesized strings that were continuously heard in any public area, a soothing sound designed to promote a sense of calm and peace.

At SousMer Underwater Resort, all the excitement was well planned and anticipated with relish, deep-ocean thrills for the well heeled.

Which was why Mary Knox was here . . .

Once she grasped the bar, it pulled her to the metal steps. There, she let go of the bar and then trudged up the three steps while burly SousMer attendants helped unsnap her helmet. One attendant gently pulled her helmet off, and Mary shook her mane of long blond hair.

The slightly fresher air of the resort billowed in.

She noticed the men's appreciative glances. But the stir she caused lasted only a moment as they hurried back to get the *next* diver out . . .

Her husband, or so they thought.

Mary Knox walked to a long bench of sculpted seats where she could—with help—unfasten the suit, shut off the communications system, and get out.

She looked back to the open water of the diving bay. She saw Cutter—"Mr. Adam Ferro" as he was known here—going through the same procedure, being pulled to the steps and then helped with the helmet.

Jack Cutter also had lots of names.

A young woman dressed in the bright turquoise spandex of SousMer came up to Mary and unpopped the fastening at the top of the EVA unit. The suit was designed for tourists—it went on and off easily, and still provided maximum protection at SousMer's not inconsiderable depth of one mile below the sea's surface.

The young woman spoke, her voice tentative . . .

"Mrs. Ferro—we lost track of you and your husband out there. We had some trouble with one of the exterior cameras. After you reached bottom, you didn't answer us—"

Mary turned to the woman. *Mrs. Ferro—now that was funny,* she thought, *as if I could actually be someone's wife.* Cutter had jammed the camera with electronic static that would appear to be just a glitch in the image processing chip.

Mary smiled. "Yes, I know. Something went wrong with my suit. I guess we couldn't hear anything. We headed north, to take a look past the resort—at the ledge."

The dive attendant looked discomfited. "You should have stayed to your EVA plan. The drop-off at the edge there is very steep. We—"

Then Cutter was there, *Mr.* Ferro, rubbing his beard.

"Anything wrong?"

Mary shook her head. "They wanted to know if"—she

4

smiled at the young woman—"if we had any *trouble* on our dive."

Cutter shook his head. "Trouble. No, nothing except for your communications going on the fritz. Some blasted interference. But—God—it was beautiful out there, the way the resort sits right next to the shelf. Made us want to jump."

Cutter laughed.

The attendant chewed her lip.

"That area is to be explored only in submersibles. The power plant is back there, Mr. Ferro. It's restricted. You knew that—"

Jack touched the attendant's shoulder.

"No damage . . . we're back safe and sound."

The attendant looked unsure, but more people were surfacing from their morning dives, more people to attend to—

The dive attendant nodded, and then she was gone.

Cutter turned to Mary. "Think she'll file a report . . . think someone will take a look outside?"

He was the worrier. Jack Cutter always worried too much, Mary thought. Always thinking too damn much. You can't think, not when you take the big chances, the big gambles.

Worrying can be dangerous.

"No, I don't. There's nothing anyone will notice, not in time. And if they do, they won't connect it to us. Now, get out of your suit."

Mary smiled, giving Jack's full beard a brush with her hand, a slight touch that they both knew promised exactly nothing.

"I could *kill* for an icy martini," Cutter said.

Harry Gooding knew the drill *cold* . . .

Three times every twenty-four hours, the SousMer maintenance crew ran an exterior inspection of the deep-sea resort. The resort was filled with redundant safety systems.

Nobody wanted to risk the lives of two hundred guests

5

and nearly twice that number of service personnel when there was—literally—no escape.

Harry Gooding eased the green maintenance sub over the dome-like top of SousMer. It was the first seating for dinner, and there were only a few diving teams still out, stragglers coming back from exploring the nearby labyrinths.

A few people were still outside the resort operating the two-person submersibles, all of them in constant communication with the resort.

But it was quiet out here now, he thought, as the high-density filament tungsten lamps on his minisub scanned the top of SousMer.

It's peaceful here, Harry thought. Not like in the resort, with the music and elegant parties and meals . . . making sure everyone got their money's worth.

To his left, Harry saw the skylight above the main dining room, the thick, clear plastic strong enough to resist twice the pressure it was under.

Ahead, on the right side of the main module of SousMer, Harry saw the pricey topside rooms, each with portholes that allowed guests to check on what or who was swimming above and around them.

But Harry was out here to check for any structural weakness . . . any irregularities. A routine maintenance check. Though Harry didn't know why it had to be done. The computer system would warn of any structural problem days before the slightest stress showed in the titanium shell of the resort.

He hovered near the power plant.

No, there was no danger here, but the surface of both the energy and air processing plants had to be examined anyway. They were also carefully monitored by the massive SousMer computer system, linked—directly by satellite—to Geoffrey Harpe's New York and London headquarters, all part of mammoth Harpe WorldWide Enterprises.

But even now, even when the plants could be virtually recreated at Engineering—miniature models exact down to the smallest detail, the smallest imperfection—there were still things that might go wrong.

Or so Harry had been told.

The message was:

Don't trust the technology.

That was the message, from RMS *Titanic* to Space Shuttle *Challenger,* to last year's disastrous Mars Expedition II.

There were so many redundancies built into all the life-support systems. And Harry Gooding, flying around the outside of the giant underwater complex, just happened to be one of those redundancies . . .

Nathan Hale Bridger—officially Captain Bridger for no more than ten days—was wondering why he had let himself be lured back to the *seaQuest DSV.*

He sat in his quarters arguing with the holographic image of Admiral Noyce's face.

"Now, Nathan—you knew that there was going to be some of this 'showboating.' The *seaQuest* represents more than merely the strong arm of UEO. It's a symbol of our determination to—"

"Bill, cut the speech making. You're not going to tell me it's actually *important* for the *seaQuest* to cruise into San Francisco Bay while this UEO energy conference is going on? The science team on board has been waiting to head up to the deep-ocean stations in Antarctica. Dr. Westphalen says that there are new discoveries being made every day."

Noyce looked away as if someone had come into the office. And when the Admiral looked back at Bridger, his face looked discomfited.

Good, thought Bridger. *Hope you feel the pinch, Bill. You suckered me into this, lured me—and it wasn't to be a PR man for the UEO.*

"Look—Nathan, just make an *appearance,* let some of the bigwigs tour *seaQuest,* let them poke around a bit, and then we'll get your team down to the Antarctic base *prontissimo.* There *have* been some amazing discoveries . . . confusing ones . . ."

Bridger hadn't read all the reports yet, but he knew that

paleoarchaeologists were saying that there would have to be changes to the various theories for the origin of life, perhaps a new theory and a whole new time scale.

Bridger raised a hand. "I know. Lucas has been snatching the security feed off EarthNet and feeding right to our scientific team. Westphalen's ready to explode, she's so eager to get down there."

Noyce took a breath.

"One week, Nate. That's all. Then, if there are no crises pending, no border disputes, no pirates raiding any settlements, then you can let Westphalen have her expedition."

Bridger shook his head. He would have liked to throw something at the virtual image of Noyce.

Except, he grinned, it would have done *virtually* no damage.

Still grinning, Bridger said, "Okay Bill. We'll make our appearance. Now let me get back to the bridge and give everyone the great news . . ."

Bridger reached out and hit a button and Noyce's face—about to say something—disappeared.

There was no question that walking onto the *seaQuest* bridge gave Captain Bridger a jolt.

After all, he had designed the *seaQuest* so that the captain's chair was at the center of the ship's systems. The chair faced the heart of *seaQuest*, the navigation and communication command centers.

It was an electric feeling to walk onto the bridge . . .

The seats for the helmsmen were a few meters ahead and—beyond them—the bank of virtual reality screens.

With the help of the WSKRS system, those screens supplied views from all around the ship, as well as views of the ship itself.

Of course, Bridger saw, Dr. Kristin Westphalen was waiting for him.

"Well—what did the Admiral say?"

Bridger's executive officer, Lieutenant Commander Jonathan Devin Ford, stood by, waiting to see exactly where the *seaQuest* was headed.

Bridger still wondered how Ford felt about turning over *seaQuest* to him. It's hard to give up a command . . . but to give up commanding *this* ship? That must have stung.

Bridger sat down in the captain's chair.

"In a minute—if you wouldn't mind—"

If a PR junket was in the offing, best to get it going . . .

"Gator, kindly put up current course." Bridger and the chief of the helm, Crocker, went way back together, back to Bridger's days on a destroyer. There had been a lot of late nights and a lot of poker games.

"Nathan, I must insist—" Westphalen pressed on with her argument. *This isn't going to be fun,* Bridger thought.

One of the VR screens displayed the current speed and course setting for *seaQuest,* a course designed to take it out of the North Atlantic. The mammoth sub was slowly heading south. Bridger had been hopeful that permission would be granted to head down to the Antarctic waters.

Well, at least now I know where we *are* going.

"Helmsmen—30 degrees port rudder . . . trim forward ballast, and take her down another 5 degrees." There would be some nasty currents ahead. A bit of depth wouldn't hurt.

"Captain Bridger," Ford said, standing to the side, "do you want a course plotted?"

Westphalen waited, as if steam were ready to blast from her ears.

"Yes, to the Panama Canal, Mr. Ford, and from there"— Bridger looked at Westphalen—"plot a course for San Francisco."

The order to plot the course meant that the bank of Cray-Apple Vbs would quickly provide any number of plotted courses, each taking into account various weather conditions current as reported by the net of orbiting LAGEOS weather satellites.

"So, Captain, my team is not to get the opportunity to look at the discoveries in the Antarctic?"

Bridger finally turned to Westphalen, now that the woman's chagrin had been vented somewhat.

"Not *now,* Dr. Westphalen. But in one week, after we

9

visit the United Earth/Ocean Organization energy conference and make a guest appearance—so to speak—*then* I've been promised that we can finally use this ship to do the science that it was intended to do."

That I *designed it to do,* thought Bridger.

Westphalen nodded, as if she were about to continue the argument, but then she turned and walked away.

Bridger looked up at Ford and grinned. "Not a happy camper, eh, Mr. Ford?" Ford smiled, though Bridger guessed that Ford also wasn't too happy at the upcoming junket.

Then Bridger checked the VR screens, now showing their new course, straight through to San Francisco Harbor.

"And neither am I, Commander."

Mary Knox slid into the silvery, low-cut evening dress. She looked up to catch Cutter ogling her.

It would be a shame if Cutter got some unprofessional ideas at this point. A deadly shame.

No telling what *I might do,* Mary thought.

"Yes?" she said.

"Er, are you ready to check the schema?"

"God—I think we pretty well have the whole place memorized. But, okay—"

Jack Cutter opened up a sleek black box. Inside there was only a small lens and a single button, making the computer look like a high-definition camera. Jack touched the button.

A logo appeared in midair, projected into the open space of the cabin. Twisting coils gradually spelled "Harpe Electronics," and then there was a verbal prompt, words emanating from the small speaker.

"Access Code and voice identification, please."

"Damn, that's too loud," Mary said.

Cutter held a small box up to his larynx and spoke. "System sound off," he said, his voice acquiring an electronic trill. And then, "Access Code 1569734."

The screen changed, and there was a general menu floating in the air, listing Files, Main Programs, DataBank, and EarthNet.

"Go ahead," Mary said.

Jack nodded. "SousMer Resort, full schema display . . ."

And then—*there* was the underwater resort floating before their eyes, a miniature report, the three-dimensional plans for the resort. But this was better than plans, because the VR image showed every change and modification done since the resort opened, the status of every mechanism.

There would be no surprises.

They were now inside the top-security level of Harpe WorldWide Enterprises, past all of Harpe's ICE—Intrusion Countermeasure Electronics—without so much as a ripple.

Some codes were better than others, and they had the best. And the vocal modulator could mimic the sound of over a dozen high-clearance Harpe executives.

"C'mon, I'm hungry," Mary Knox said. She slipped into a pair of heels and started brushing her hair.

"Interior life-support systems," Jack said, and the VR image of SousMer seemed to open up, liquid, beautiful to look at. Mary saw the engineering decks of the resort, where the air was processed, the energy generated.

"Show all pathways," Cutter said.

Then a bright red, filament-thin line highlighted all the paths to the engineering level.

All so familiar to Mary . . .

For the past two days she and Jack had tested the entrance to each crawl space, each engineering duct, until they thought they knew these paths almost as well as the computer.

"Show the least secure path," Cutter said, double-checking that nothing had changed.

Mary looked at him. He worries too much, she thought.

And then there was only one red path, leading from the pool and exercise area, a duct that trailed along the bottom of the resort, right into Engineering.

Jack reached out and touched the image, his hand bathed in the red. And then his fingers played with the metallic gray and green of the resort.

"That's it then," he said. "That's our path."

Jack reached out to shut the machine off—but Mary's hand stopped him.

She shook her head. God, he could be dense sometimes. She spoke evenly. "You're forgetting something . . ."

Jack nodded. "Oh." Then, "Erase all evidence of inquiry."

There was a blip as if the command had some trouble being processed. The VR image flickered and then stabilized again. Then—

"System off."

Mary smiled at Jack.

"Guess it's showtime, Jack. Let me get my face on . . . while *you* get the explosives . . ."

Even Jack Cutter laughed at that.

CHAPTER 2

God—now, what in the world is that?

Harry Gooding pulled back on the stick of the minisub. The sub slowed and finally hovered over the left side of the energy plant.

He rubbed at his chin, feeling the stubble, and then he reached out to aim an exterior spotlight down at the wall of the plant.

Damn—there's something stuck on the side of the wall there, Harry thought. *Stuck right to the side of the plant. Something small, and round—*

Harry spoke to himself.

"Some kind of fish. That's what it is." He nodded. "It must be some kind of sucker fish."

Gooding wasn't terribly knowledgeable about SousMer's neighbors a mile down. There were times when he had to pilot his sub through a bunch of tiger sharks and he'd go into a cold sweat . . . thinking that the sharks would circle his mini-sub and chew right through the metal and plastic.

His coworkers joked, "Don't worry, Harry—one taste and they'll spit you right out."

13

Very funny—still, Harry didn't like the sharks.

I wonder, he thought . . . *can I get the sub a bit closer? Scare the thing off.*

Harry Gooding grabbed the stick and, giving the twin rear props a bit more power, tried to edge close to the energy module. He gained a few feet and then—damn, he had to back off, afraid of ramming the wall.

That would be great, he thought, *terrific, smash into the wall, dent it, and good-bye, Harry Gooding.*

He ended up with the sub pretty much where he had started from. Once again, he trained the light on the object stuck to the underside of the module's wall.

It's some kind of animal, that's what it is.

Still—

If he filed a report, a team would have to come out and do a close-up examination. *And,* thought Harry, *I'd have to be on that team.*

"Go on," he said to the sucker fish. "Get the hell out of here." He blinked, half-expecting the fish, the ray, whatever it was, to dart suddenly away to the safety of one of the nearby labyrinths.

"Go bite one of the tourists."

A light started blinking on his console, signaling that he'd reached the halfway point of his fuel.

Gooding nodded. "It's nothing," he said, and he peeled away, putting the object behind him . . .

"Mrs. Ferro, you haven't touched your salmon. Not hungry tonight?"

Mary looked over at her dinner companion, Dr. Richard Ernst. The young scientist had been attentive to her since his arrival at SousMer yesterday, and tonight her slinky dress only assured that his attentions would continue.

Mr. Ferro sat across from her, still wolfing down the shrimp and oysters. He was having no difficulty pulling off his part.

"The salmon really is excellent," Ernst said, and Mary felt the flirtatious undertones to his repartee. "It's . . . delicious."

14

She smiled, playing along with him. The previous night, at the lavish cocktail hour, Ernst had told her about his area of expertise—paleobiology and underwater microbial colonies.

How fascinating . . .

Still, this role worked well—the bored, beautiful wife married to a wealthy ingrate . . . flirting with the handsome scientist.

With more time, she could have made even more interesting use of the scientist. But—a pity—the clock was running.

Mary saw Cutter, her erstwhile husband, reach for a glass of champagne. She cleared her throat, and when he took no notice, Mary spoke:

"Honey, don't you think that you've had enough?"

And, just about to sip, Jack Cutter stopped and glared at his "wife."

Mary looked away, feigning embarrassment.

Then she looked over to the woman sitting close to her husband. A pretty woman, in her late thirties, with short blond hair and intelligent blue eyes. Her name was Terry McShane, and she said she was a writer.

And Mary Knox, with that sense that had more than once saved her life, *knew* that McShane was lying. It was the one thing that made her uneasy tonight.

She saw the way McShane looked around the grand dining room, taking in the glittery guests in fancy clothes, people eating the succulent salmon while hungry sharks swam past the side portholes. There were happy executives with wives, husbands, mistresses, or rent-a-hunks on their arms, dancing to the smooth string orchestra playing every sappy song from the past forty years.

Mary looked at Terry McShane and knew—she wasn't here on vacation.

So what *was* she here for?

"Care to dance?" Ernst asked Mary. "I mean," he said loudly, "if Mr. Ferro wouldn't mind."

Cutter, ever the *bon homme,* waved her away, only now starting to sloppily dig into his main course.

15

On the dance floor, Ernst held her close, then closer—and Mary felt herself wishing that her stay at SousMer might last just a bit longer.

"This you have to see."

Bridger waited. Lucas Wolenczak, resident computer tech and cybernet surfer of *seaQuest,* had begged Bridger to come to the communication station. Bridger noticed that Lucas was still wearing his 2014 World Champion Marlins cap. The boy was loyal if nothing else . . .

"Thought the cap was gone . . . until the Marlins started winning again?"

Lucas looked up at Bridger and said, in perfect seriousness, "You gotta believe, Captain. But wait a minute."

Darwin was swimming back and forth in the main tank near the communications center. From here, the dolphin could swim to passageways leading to everywhere from the moon pool to the science labs.

The dolphin looked mighty eager, Bridger thought, as if he were about to be tossed a tub of herring.

"You got Darwin excited." Bridger watched Darwin, still not used to the fact that the dolphin could communicate, albeit in short sentence fragments. "Do you know what Lucas is up to, Dar?"

Bridger heard a series of trill-like cheeps, and then the speaker, the computer translating the signals.

"We have surprise for you."

Bridger laughed. "Good, I could use a nice surprise."

Lucas hit some buttons on the side console, and he was immediately connected with the main bank of Cray-Apple Vbs. "I made some modifications to Darwin's communication program."

"I was impressed enough with what Darwin could do . . ."

"Okay—just a minute. There," Lucas said. "He's ready."

"Ready for what?"

Lucas turned to the dolphin. "Darwin, do you see any problem with our current course?"

Darwin flipped around excitedly. "There is a storm . . . It has changed direction."

"What? How could he—"

Lucas grinned. "Let's check up on him."

Lucas hit some keys, and a VR display window above the dolphin showed a live satellite picture of the Caribbean, stretching from Cuba on down past Aruba. And there, sitting off to the east, was a nasty-looking swirl.

"Looks like the tropical storm started developing after you set your course, Captain. Though at the klicks we're making, we'll probably beat it to the Canal. If you hurry . . ."

"Yes, but how did Darwin know about the storm?"

Darwin did a loop, obviously pleased with himself.

"*That's* my modification . . . Darwin can access the ship's computer system, anything from navigation and targeting to getting information from EarthNet, including the latest from the LAGEOS satellites."

Darwin chirped, and the speaker carried the translation, the synthesized voice that Bridger now accepted indisputably as Darwin's . . . "I can *see* the ship."

"And he understands what he sees?" Bridger asked.

"He's a very quick study."

Bridger nodded. Well, that should make Darwin even more helpful. But there was something that worried Bridger.

"Great. Go play now, Darwin."

The dolphin vanished down the clear Plexiglas tube that ran to the science wing.

It worried Bridger . . . Was this too much to dump on Darwin? Darwin had said, "I like it here . . . want to stay." And that was one of the reasons Bridger had taken the command.

But maybe Darwin didn't know what was good for him.

"Sir—"

Bridger turned and saw his exec, Lieutenant Commander Ford, standing behind him.

"We got a download about a hurricane system beginning at 20 degrees south and 110 degrees east, heading north at 30 klicks—and the system's picking up speed, sir."

Lucas looked at Bridger, the computer whiz kid grinning broadly.

"I already *know,* Commander. All ahead full on our present course, and we'll probably beat the bumpy weather."

Ford looked confused, but he saluted and returned to the bridge. And Captain Bridger patted Lucas's shoulder and left for his cabin.

It wouldn't hurt to catch forty winks.

He still missed his naps back on the island, when the afternoon sun grew hot and civilization was a thousand miles away . . .

On cue, Cutter started talking loudly. Mary saw him looking around.

"Oh, dear," she said, close to Dr. Ernst's ear. "I'm afraid my husband's about to make a scene."

Ernst whispered back into her ear.

"Can I escort you somewhere?"

A stingray glided overhead, its white underbelly catching the brilliant light of the dining room.

Mary looked up at Ernst and smiled. "No. I'm afraid I'd better go back—"

But then Cutter was standing there, slurring his words.

"D-do you mind? I-I'd like to dance with my wife. If—you *wouldn't* mind."

Mary gave Ernst's hand a squeeze, reassuring, promising, and then backed away.

"Adam, please. You've had too much to drink and—"

Cutter wobbled back and forth as if the stationary resort were really a liner wobbling in the stormy Atlantic.

"So—you *don't* want to dance with me, with your own husban'?"

Mary looked at Ernst, and then at the other people at her table, all of them looking on with sympathy.

"We'd better go back to our suite. I think—"

She took Cutter's arm and he yanked it away. But Mary was able to grab his elbow again and whisper to him, soothing him. At least, that's what it was supposed to look like . . .

She walked Cutter, wobbling, drunken, out of the dining room, the men eyeing her while the women counted their blessings.

They were in the main hallway of SousMer.

"Okay, good work, Cutter. I think you can straighten up now."

"*Whas a mata?* C'mon, baby, give me a little kiss . . ." Cutter laughed, leaning into her.

"Stop it. We're on schedule. Let's keep it that way."

And immediately Cutter was sober. "You're no fun anymore."

"Ready?" she said.

Cutter nodded.

Together they walked down the hallway and followed the elegant stairs that curved under another large porthole, showing the sea outside.

They came to another hallway with sleek metal walls, and as rehearsed, they followed that to the Olympic pool and the exercise room.

A burly attendant was closing up poolside chairs.

That's unexpected, Mary thought. No one should be here now . . . but it wasn't a big problem.

The attendant looked up when he saw the two people enter the pool area. "Sorry, folks. But the pool is closed for the evening."

Mary smiled, walking closer to the man. "That's okay. We're just exploring."

The man smiled. "I'm afraid that you have to leave. I'm only cleaning up here. It's actually—"

Mary smiled. She reached into her handbag and pulled out an stun gun, an odd-shaped gun that looked more like a hand weight. The man looked confused, probably not recognizing exactly what she had in her hand.

So, she thought, he'd be *surprised*. The gun could stun or kill, depending on the setting.

This one was set to kill.

Mary pulled the trigger, and it fired an electrically charged dart right at the attendant's chest. It hit, and the man's eyes

19

bugged out. He tumbled backward into the pool.

"God—was that necessary?" Cutter asked.

Mary turned to him. "Don't wimp out on me, Jack."

She hurried past the pool to the expansive exercise area, filled with machines, and into a storage room filled with chemicals and towels.

Inside the room, Cutter threw the light switch. They moved quickly now—Mary was glad that this was just as they had rehearsed it.

Except for the dead man in the pool . . . Oh, well, even the best plans have to be changed.

And, just as the VR plans of the resort had shown, there it was . . .

A metal grate on one wall.

"There you go, Cutter. Get moving."

Cutter easily popped the grate out, ripping the wire mesh free from the screws that held it to the opening.

"This opening looks kind of small," he said.

"The plans show that there's plenty of room."

Cutter nodded, and then dug into his coat pocket. He pulled out a small greenish packet. The explosive looked like Plasticine, a colored doughlike substance. The organic explosive had been undetected by SousMer's security system . . . They could have sneaked pounds of the stuff into the resort.

"And the timer?" Mary said.

Cutter dug into his other pocket and pulled out a small round object the size of a tiny watch battery. The microchip contained the timer and the igniter, a small program to set off the explosive.

Cutter grinned. "All set."

"Then get going," Mary said, and she turned to keep watch while Cutter crawled into the hole.

Harry sat in the staff cafeteria, watching one of the overhead VidDisplays. The cafeteria VR screens weren't state-of-the-art, but still the sitcom had a nice 3-D feel to it.

One of the other maintenance people, Billy Carullo, sat

down next to him, his tray loaded with two semibeef cheeseburgers and what might have been honest-to-God onion rings.

"Hey, I saw this one," Carullo said. "The husband says he lost his access code, but his wife thinks he's buying presents for a girlfriend. Duh . . ."

Harry looked at Carullo. "Thanks for the story, Carullo. Guess I don't have to watch it now."

"Oh, hey man, sorry." Carullo held out his platter of onion rings. "Want one?"

Harry shook his head. "Hey, Carullo. Tell me, you ever go outside and see something, some fish or something, stuck to the side of one of the tanks?"

Carullo took a giant bite of one of the mostly-soy burgers, catsup and melted cheese drooling from the side.

"What? What are you talking about?"

Harry looked around. It wouldn't be great if a supervisor overheard this conversation. "You know, did you ever see some kind of sucker fish thing, stuck to the side—?"

Carullo laughed, his mouth still full.

"Hey, I don't know *what* you're talking about." He paused before his next bite. "You saw something out there, something stuck to one of the modules?"

Harry nodded. "I-I think it was a fish."

"And you *didn't* report it to Systems Management?"

Harry chewed his lip. "I didn't think it was anything. I didn't want to make us go out there . . . for some dumb fish . . ."

Carullo shook his head. "Buddy, if I were you, I'd let whoever's on duty know that you forgot to mention something from your last go-round. And I'd do it now."

Harry nodded, trying to think of an excuse, wondering if this would mean that he'd be fired. Then it would be back to hiring out free-lance to some of the wildcat deep-sea mines. Bad hours, dangerous conditions, and worse pay . . .

But Harry didn't know that that would be the least of his problems.

Mary waited . . .

She heard a sound by the locked doors that led from the pool out to the pool bar and game room. But the pool bar was closed—and no one came into the closed pool.

Good thing too; otherwise she'd have had to kill someone else.

She leaned next to the grating and heard Jack grunting, crawling toward the engineering wing of the resort, the place where the power was managed, where the air was processed—the heart of the resort.

Then, after a while, she couldn't hear Cutter anymore. There was more waiting, and then, again, more grunting, until Mary could lean in and see Cutter wriggling out backward.

She backed away and let him slide out.

"Everything okay?"

Cutter was red-faced from the exertion.

"I put it right next to the engineering room grate. It will blow the damn place to pieces."

His grin had a stupidity to it that Mary found repellant.

"Good—let's get to a VidScreen and watch the show. It's almost time . . ."

They left, ignoring the attendant floating facedown, as if he were studying the bottom of the pool.

CHAPTER 3

Bridger flopped into his bunk, clothes on, thinking:

Since the UEO has turned us into a cruise ship, a tourist attraction, the SS Public Relations, *I might as well catch some Zs.*

Because—nothing eventful is in the offing.

Bridger rubbed his eyes. The *seaQuest* was a silent ship. A deep hum, barely audible, was the only indication that it was moving, the twin hydrojets making the mammoth sub move along at a steady 110 klicks an hour. Pushed, it could cruise at a steady 160 knots.

Bridger stared at the ceiling of his cabin.

He thought that maybe his being here was all a mistake. Admiral Noyce had sneaked Darwin onto the *seaQuest*, and Darwin—able to talk through electronic wizardry—had said that he wanted to stay on the sub.

But, Bridger thought, *I'm not married to Darwin. The dolphin could have stayed and enjoyed his new role as an ensign. And I could have stayed on the island.*

Should *have stayed on the island . . .*

With that, he fell asleep.

▲   ▲   ▲

Mary was quickly out of her tight dinner dress and into a
super-thin kelvar outfit before Cutter even noticed. He was
fiddling with the computer.

"What's wrong?" she said.

Cuter shook his head. "Nothing. I'm having a bit of trouble getting—"

Then the machine came on and projected a commercial
vid station into the air. It was a sitcom, and Cutter laughed.

Loves his sitcoms, Mary guessed.

"This station okay?" Cutter said, as if feeling her disap-
proval.

"Doesn't matter," Mary said. Any station would do, any
channel, any network. In a few minutes, it wouldn't matter
what anyone was watching . . . anywhere.

Cutter laughed again and Mary shook her head.

It wouldn't matter . . . because—

Rafael Vargas was sitting off the Mariana Trench,
in his modified Skipjack—a very fast sub and armed to the
teeth—waiting.

Mary wished he was here. Maybe he'd tell her that it
was okay to put her stun gun up against Jack Cutter's stupid head and fire away while he was in mid-laugh.

But Cutter knew all about the new organic explosives,
and all about the microdetonators, chip fuses, wireless trig-
gers.

He was important. He had his role—but his part was
almost done.

Cutter still wasn't dressed in his kelvar suit.

"Don't you think you should get ready?" she said.

"Ha," Cutter laughed at the screen floating in midair.
"You ever see this? It's really—"

Mary looked at her Orlande dive watch, good to ten thousand feet. Who knew, she thought . . . Before this was all
over, that specification might just have to get tested.

It was only minutes away . . . seconds . . .

"Get ready, Cutter. It's coming on right—"

There was a blip, and the three-dimensional sitcom vanished, leaving a black hole laced with multicolored specks.

Mary imagined everyone's concern.

Call the TeleNet SysOp, dear. Something's wrong.

But before the world's couch potatoes could leave their perches—wondering, *Where's my game show, where's my movie, where's my talk show*—the interlaced communications network picked up *another* signal, traveling the emergency network established by the UEO in 2016.

And there was Rafael Vargas, a familiar visage to the world's governments, any one of which would gladly have had him terminated outright, no questions asked.

This was thrilling.

"Good evening," Rafael said. He had dark eyes, tanned skin, and his smile—so insolent as to be delicious—gave Mary a thrill.

"Let me apologize for interrupting your programs"—the smile broadened—"around the world." He paused, and then a three-dimensional representation of SousMer appeared next to him, as recognizable as the Universal World Park in Southern California. SousMer was the non-plus-ultra of expensive vacations.

And the price was about to go up.

"I regret to inform the guests and staff of SousMer that I have planted a series of explosives, hidden and undetectable, throughout the complex."

Mary looked at Cutter, still struggling to fit his gut into his large kelvar suit.

"God, he's got balls," Cutter said.

Mary had listened to the tape before coming to SousMer; she had helped Rafael script it, reworking each line to make sure that it carried full weight.

Yes, she thought, *yes, Rafael certainly does have balls . . .*

It was sunset on the island, and Bridger saw Barbara walking on the beach. Though he knew this was a dream, only another cruel dream, he couldn't resist walking up to her.

She wore one of his denim shirts tied up so casually, so alluringly. A pair of cutoff jeans, bare feet. She turned and saw him.

In the dream, he felt as if he had something to tell her, and something very important to ask her.

He ran now, his feet crunching on the dry, crystalline sand. He called to her, and she waved, the late afternoon breeze catching her hair, playing with it.

And now came the part that felt familiar. He felt himself thinking, hoping, begging. Please, *don't let this be a dream. Let everything else be the dream, everything else that happened, her sickness, her death—so sudden that there had been no time to say good-bye . . .*

Let all *that* be the dream.

"Barbara," he said.

She kept waving. And—closer now—he saw her tanned stomach, the skin brown, her blue eyes catching the setting sun.

And he was there, with her again.

Not a dream, not a dream, it must be—

He remembered what he had to tell her.

It was about their son. It came to him. The bad news he had. How their son was dead, how he had died playing war in Antarctica. "You'd be proud of him," his captain had said, but Bridger shook his head and thought, *No, you don't understand. With him gone, there's nothing.*

In the dream, he spoke to Barbara, telling her.

"He's gone. Our son—"

But the breeze stopped. The orange sunlight began to fade so quickly. Clouds filled the sky, and Bridger looked around, thinking. *That never happens here. Not on the island. No clouds, no rain, not now—*

And Barbara looked around too, disturbed—as if she also knew that this was a dream. And she said, quietly, softly . . .

"Nate, I . . . miss you."

Bridger started crying, heaving in his dream, crying in his cabin, digging at his pillow, aboard the *seaQuest* . . .

"What the f—"

Harry Gooding's companion stood up. A deadly silence filled the cafeteria. Everyone was watching the VidScreen,

26

listening to world famous terrorist Rafael Vargas speak quietly about the place that they happened to be in, a mile under the water . . .

"The explosives have been placed both inside and outside SousMer. In fact, we have even placed certain charges to serve as demonstration should Geoffrey Harpe of Harpe WorldWide Enterprises or any authorities require proof that this threat is in deadly earnest."

Then—a neat touch—a portion of the 3-D resort dancing in front of Rafael *exploded* with a noisy bang and virtual smoke that swirled about him.

Mary heard noises outside her cabin. People scrambling, panicking. Some perhaps heading toward the twin sub bays of SousMer.

That headlong rush should end in a moment, Mary knew.

"There can be no escape from the resort," Rafael continued. "Should any sub escape attempt be made by anyone, I will destroy a section of the resort . . ."

Each module of the resort could exist separately, Mary knew from the schematics. There were watertight doors and all sorts of emergency provisions.

But all of the modules were linked to and depended on the power plant and oxygen system. Emergency supplies of energy and air would last only a short time.

Mary grinned. There were a lot of disappointed fat cats packing overnight bags even as Rafael spoke.

But they wouldn't get far.

The clouds turned into a gray ceiling, and then there was a ringing sound, a high-pitched electronic noise above the hum, above the sound of *seaQuest* gliding through the water.

And a voice.

"Captain . . . Captain Bridger." And this world, the real world, was back.

Bridger's exec, Commander Ford, stood there.

"Captain, we're picking up something that you should see." Bridger's VR screen was linked with all the ship's systems, and it could download from any station on the Net if the sub wasn't down too deep.

Ford didn't wait for permission to turn on the screen.

Bridger rubbed his face, feeling the wet sheen on his cheeks, that part of the dream real enough.

On the screen he saw a man talking . . . while a hologram of Geoffrey Harpe's SousMer resort floated to the man's side.

Bridger blinked and listened . . .

"Any attempt to escape the resort, in a submersible or by EVA suit, will trigger an explosion. I will be monitoring the entire resort." Rafael paused.

Bit of an overstatement there, Mary thought, but who'd know?

Now the resort ominously disappeared from the screen.

"And what do we want? Not much . . . only a hundred million in gold bullion to be dropped in the Pacific Ocean, at 13 degrees, 25 minutes north, and 145 degrees, 33 minutes east. An exact map is being downloaded to all the primary data bases as I speak. The bullion is to be dropped within the next twenty-four hours. There should be no ship of any kind within a hundred miles of the drop range."

Mary knew that Rafael was sitting there right now, waiting. And after the drop, he'd get the gold aboard his Skipjack and hide in the canyons and valleys of the trench. With a hundred-mile arc, he'd have no trouble getting out.

Mary imagined the world listening to this message, the calls from the U.S. President's office as she tried to track down Harpe, and the council of the UEO trying to decide if they'd pay. Or rather, if they'd make Harpe pay.

They might need some convincing.

The on-screen map of the Pacific showed the drop zone.

"There will be no further messages. Unless confirmation is received within the next sixty minutes, I will detonate one of the explosives . . ."

"You mean *I* will," Cutter said.

Rafael smiled ". . . to demonstrate our sincerity. Other

explosions will follow in course, until the drop is confirmed via a message on the Net. And remember—"

Here it was, Mary thought. The big finish.

SousMer was back on the screen again.

"If the gold is not dropped in"—Rafael looked down at his watch, as if this were love—"exactly twenty-three hours and forty-four minutes—" He paused.

The on-screen resort exploded . . . while Rafael's smile remained, like the Cheshire cat's.

The sitcom came back on, and Harry Gooding stared at the show, his mouth open.

"Son of a bitch," Billy Carullo said to Harry. "This is great, this is damn terrific. We're hostages and we get to die if Harpe doesn't cough up a hundred million."

Harry looked around. The cafeteria was abuzz with noise. Another face appeared on the screen, rudely pushing aside the sitcom.

"All SousMer staff immediately report to your supervisor."

Right, thought Harry, who had been working up the chutzpah to tell someone what he had seen stuck to the side of the power station.

Carullo turned to him. "Hey, Harry—you don't think that thing you saw, the—"

"Fish," Harry offered. "It was a *fish* . . . "

Carullo shook his head. "You don't think that it might be one of the—"

Oh, this was bad, real bad. Forget losing a job. This was about people's lives. *My life,* Harry thought. And—for the moment—Harry Gooding accepted all the responsibility for the predicament SousMer found itself in.

"Now, that's an interesting situation," Bridger said. "A billion dollar resort, five hundred, maybe six hundred people's lives versus a hundred million from Harpe's coffers. Kinda spoils his day."

"Sir—you think he'll pay up?"

Bridger swung around on his cot. "Oh, I would say he'll

have to, Mr. Ford. It might be a bluff, but how can they test it?"

Then Bridger had the thought that, hell, they *might* just do that. There was no discounting anyone's stupidity, not when money was involved.

Ford still stood there, as if waiting for something.

"Er, thanks for waking me up, Mr. Ford. Keep me posted as to what's going on. Right now, I want to have a quick shower . . ."

"Captain . . ." Ford paused. "Do you thing the UEO will want us to get involved?"

Bridger was rubbing his chin, feeling the stubble, longing for his beard, the loss of which signaled that the real world was far away.

He looked up at Ford, who was offering a concept that hadn't occurred to Bridger.

"What's that, Commander?"

"Sir, it's only that we're within cruising distance of the resort. I don't know what action the UEO might want to take."

"Well, don't ask, keep our course. Harpe's got the money—"

Bridger caught himself, caught the edge to his voice. Harpe and he went way back. But their parting of the ways couldn't have been more severe.

"Let him buy his way out of this—like he has everything else in his life."

Ford nodded. "Right, sir," he said and stepped out of the cabin.

Bridger stood up and stretched. It would be interesting to follow this negotiation, he thought, while they leisurely cruised to Panama. He walked to the shower in the corner of the comfortable stateroom.

Then his VidScreen signaled an incoming personal message.

A soft tone, followed by Communication Officer Bachmann.

"Captain, we've got a private communication link coming in for you from Nor-Pac UEO."

Bridger shook his head.

"Can't it wait?" Bridger felt grimy; the hot shower would feel so good.

"Captain—it's Admiral Noyce."

Bridger laughed.

Thinking: *How come my exec saw this coming and I didn't?*

Boy . . . am I rusty or what?

"So," Cutter said, "we wait?"

Mary nodded. "For about forty-five minutes, and then we give everyone here a sample of your expertise."

Mary checked both their stun guns while Cutter walked back and forth in the small cabin.

At the SousMer maintenance station, the computers were scanning the complex.

Not my department, Harry Gooding thought. *I don't understand computers.* He saw his chief though, Sachio Kodei, studying the monitors, snapping orders at a crew.

"Keep screen one on life-support. Now bring up the data on guest quarters on screen two. Okay, okay—now—"

The smell of fear in the electronic nerve center of the resort was enough to make Harry sick.

"Chief," he said, then realizing he had said it much too quietly, he cleared his throat. "Chief—"

Kodei turned to him.

"Harry—what is it, Harry? We can't use you, you know. No one's going outside. Didn't you hear . . ."

Harry edged closer. He didn't want the room full of technicians to hear.

"I thought . . . I should tell you something."

He scratched the back of his neck.

Kodei studied him with his glasses low on his nose, wrinkling his face.

Harry cleared his throat again. "I saw something last time out."

Kodei's face started to curl into a frown.

"On one of the power plant modules. Plant two."

31

Kodei didn't turn away. "Put plant two on screen four," the chief engineer said without turning away.

This wasn't going well, Harry thought. *No, I think I'm about to make a sudden, involuntary career change.*

"I saw something stuck to the underside of plant two. It looked like a fish. But now—"

An exterior camera showed the plant, but the shot didn't show the area where Harry had seen his sucker fish.

"I-I thought it was a sucker fish. But now I don't know . . ."

Kodei turned to one of the technicians. "When did that camera go off-line?"

"About five hours ago. We lost image for about ten minutes."

"Damn," Kodei said, and he whipped out a TeleCom unit while Harry wished he could melt into the floor.

CHAPTER 4

"What's the problem, Bill?" Bridger said. "Harpe pays up and the UEO catches them later?"

Bridger saw Bill Noyce look away for a moment, as if someone off-screen had said something to him. Then the Admiral nodded.

And Bridger thought:

There's no way that the seaQuest *should get involved in this. If the explosives are there, sitting with remote detonators, there's nothing that can be done—*

"Nathan—here's the situation. There are some very important people down there. Important people from major business interests, some very important government people . . ."

Who, Bridger guessed, were supposed to be somewhere else . . .

"More the reason to pay up quickly . . . and then try to find Vargas."

Noyce shook his head. "We've contacted Harpe. There's no problem. He's not very happy, but he can get the bullion in place and fly it out to the drop zone within the time limit—"

"So what's the—?"

There was a knock at Bridger's cabin door.

"Sorry, Bill. Wait a minute." Bridger looked to the door. "Come in."

Chief Engineer Katherine Hitchcock was at the door. "Oh, sorry, Captain. Didn't know you were busy—"

"What is it?"

Hitchcock had the door partly closed again. "Oh, Captain, I wanted to know if it's okay if we deployed WSKRS during our run to Panama . . . to check out Wolenczak's modifications . . ."

Modifications? Darwin's modifications? Bridger wondered.

He nodded. "Sure," and once again felt that while the *seaQuest* might have been his once, he had a hell of lot of catching up to do.

From his UEO office in California, Noyce was smiling. "Seems like you're settling in nicely, Nathan."

"Playing catch-up is more like it."

"Nate—we can get the gold there. But here's the problem. We think—"

Noyce took a breath.

He proceeded to tell Bridger what the *real* problem was.

Mary walked over to Cutter's minicomputer console and shut the video screen off. The sitcom floating in the middle of the room disappeared.

"Hey—" Cutter protested.

"We're behind schedule, Cutter. And you're not fully suited up yet."

Cutter still hadn't put on the protective vest that fit over the kelvar jacket. It was possible that no one would get to take a shot at them, but if they caught some heat, it wouldn't bother them at all with all this armor.

"Okay," Cutter said, groaning. "Except this stuff is so damn tight."

Mary shook her head. "Suck it in, Cutter. You've got ten minutes until show time."

Cutter shook his head. "I don't get it. Why do we have to—?"

34

She put a finger to his lips.

"Don't ask too many questions." She grinned. "You may not like the answers . . ."

And Jack Cutter zipped up his vest.

Terry McShane left the main dining room. She saw the SousMer staff struggling to keep everyone calm, telling them that everything was "okay." The resort director announced on the speakers that even now the UEO was making arrangements to pay off the terrorists.

Truth or BS? McShane guessed that nothing had been decided. Not yet—

But that's not what worried her.

She wandered down toward the control center of SousMer, toward the engineering and life-support facilities, off-limits to guests.

SousMer staff ran through the carpeted hallway, their faces grim, set. And she thought that this was what it must have been like on the *Titanic* when the crew knew how bad things were . . . while the passengers only thought that there had been a slight adjustment in their travel schedule.

I've got to get to a computer station, McShane thought, looking at the various open rooms.

Got to get to a computer.

And let the UEO know where I am . . .

Dr. Richard Ernst huddled in the corner of the SousMer Seven Seas Lounge. The garish blue-green mother-of-pearl effect on the walls and ceiling made him feel as if he were already in the water.

Already drowning.

It's not so good to have too much of an imagination, he thought. Not good to sit here and imagine an explosion . . . hitting anywhere, and the water rushing in, washing people down the hallways, while others ran ahead of the rushing water, screaming.

Or maybe—he wasn't sure—the explosives would blow a hole in the resort and the pressure would crush the complex like a Fabergé egg. That, at least, would be fast.

Ernst looked up at the bartender.

The bartender was gone, but that didn't matter. Under the circumstances, a bartender wasn't necessary. Ernst got up shakily, walked behind the bar, and dug out a bottle of Glenfiddich scotch from the counter. He poured a tumbler half full, and then carried the glass of amber liquid back to his chair.

Please, he thought while slugging the scotch.

He begged for his life to a power that at any other time in his life he would have scoffed at.

For Dr. Richard Ernst, there had been only science. And science couldn't help him much now . . .

"Nathan, we think that once the gold is dropped and picked up, they may still blow SousMer."

"Christ." Bridger rubbed his chin, feeling for his phantom beard. He missed it. "What do you mean . . . they may still blow the resort?"

Bridger's cabin felt small to him and the air—cleaned and refreshed steadily—now tasted stale, bitter . . .

"Just that . . . once they get the gold, we think that they'll set off the explosions anyway."

"What on earth for?"

"We're not sure. I mean, Nathan, we're *guessing* here. But our best political crisis simulations all project that the terrorist action is sponsored by one of the big independent deep-sea mining concerns, or maybe one of the pirate combines."

"I still don't get it—"

"Since the united action of the UEO, laws have been enforced, skirmishes controlled . . . and there's been peace. And you know that the independent mining cartels, with their private sub fleets—modified and heavily armed, mind you—have been controlled. But some of them don't like the new system. They develop a way to embarrass the UEO, distract it, and maybe bring the whole shaky alliance tumbling down."

Bridger shook his head. Six hundred people, ransomed and then killed anyway.

He took a breath.

"So what do you want me to do, Bill?" Bridger regretted the question the minute he voiced it.

Noyce shifted in his seat. "Nathan, we have someone inside. I haven't heard from her yet—but I expect to. But we've gotten some information on a possible—I stress *possible*—location of one of the charges."

"Yes, and if anyone goes near it, it will be detonated. So how does that—?"

"Perhaps—but that's not all. We think that they're *still* there."

"What? Who's still there?"

"We have good reason to believe that whoever planted the charges, inside and outside the complex, whatever—we *think* that they're still there."

"And what makes you say that?"

"We have a report . . . An outside maintenance person spotted something, maybe an explosive, on his last inspection. Not only that, they've been able to pinpoint when it was planted. The cameras went down. A glitch in the system . . . or so they thought."

"They're still there— What are these people running? A suicide mission?"

"I doubt it. No, if they're still there, they'll be getting out soon. I think—"

Bridger saw Noyce look to the side. Someone handed him a piece of paper. Was he getting more information? Bridger thought. And, more importantly, was he telling Bridger everything he knew?

Noyce skimmed the sheet of paper, then looked back at Bridger.

"The UEO thinks we have a window of opportunity here, Nathan. If the terrorists are still there, the UEO thinks . . ."

Here it comes . . .

". . . that the *seaQuest* can play a role."

"And what the hell role is that?"

"Nathan, *seaQuest* has the ability to monitor the resort, scan it for any irregularities. You might even get a team into the resort—without anyone detecting."

"I'm not so sure about that."

"You've got the WSKRS data, Darwin, the entire resources of the Net. Nate, I want to patch you directly through to the command center at the resort. If the terrorists are still there, maybe you can save the six hundred people a mile deep."

Sure, Bridger thought. And he wondered if Noyce had considered something else. Maybe the terrorists *wanted* the *seaQuest* to get involved. What better way to embarrass the UEO but to bring its flagship down?

But Bridger didn't say anything. He was only glad that he had taken that catnap, bad dream and all . . . because now it might be a long time before he got some sleep.

"Certainly, everything is in motion," Geoffrey Harpe said, speaking on the phone.

His guests were still enjoying the late afternoon Hawaiian sunshine, sipping exotic drinks by the pool, eating some of Chef Moritani's succulent swordfish drenched in a tangy pineapple sauce.

There was no need to interrupt the party.

But the fun, for Harpe, was over. SousMer was to have been the first in a chain of underwater resorts, offering the wealthy every thrill of this new era of underwater exploration.

Now it appeared that the thrills might be getting way out of hand.

Now all of Harpe's plans were threatened.

"You may send the message that I will have the bullion in the air by . . ."

Harpe checked his watch. It was the middle of the night in Switzerland, but one call to Harpe's European executives would get the wheels rolling very quickly. "I imagine that I can have the gold out of Lausanne airport by, say, four A.M., Swiss time."

The voice on the other end sounded relieved. Harpe's first contact had been with Admiral Noyce himself. No love lost there, Harpe knew. But Noyce was now busy dealing with the crisis—and Harpe had to deal with Noyce's aide.

The gold was no problem. And Harpe guessed that this UEO functionary wasn't used to someone who could make things happen—just like *that*.

"From there the plane will fly to Hong Kong, and the gold will be loaded onto a C-137 transport. The C-137 will fly directly to the drop zone." Harpe paused. "So—there won't be any problem at my end."

Harpe looked out the giant plate-glass window at his guests, enjoying the sun, the drinks, the gentle jazz. He envied their lack of troubles. He shook his head. This party had been expensive before . . . but now the cost had gone up to a hundred million dollars.

"Oh," Harpe said, "there is one thing. I'd like to know what steps the UEO will be taking to recover my bullion."

Later, Harpe knew that he could start his own private "inquiries." There were plenty of nasty free-lance investigators who could track down the gold and—with enough firepower and luck—recover it. But he wanted to hear what the UEO had planned.

And that's when he listened as Admiral Noyce's aide, a former member of Britain's M5 Intelligence unit, delivered the news that the scenario in progress could, in fact, take a much worse turn.

That the payoff might not end the business.

Now the party was really ruined for Harpe.

Cutter sat on his bunk.

Mary saw him sweating under the weight of so much leathery armor—or maybe he was sweating simply because this was too damn nerve-racking.

It was funny, Mary thought, that someone whose expertise was handling highly volatile explosives could be so *nervous*.

"There it is," Cutter said. He looked up at Mary. "God, yes! The confirmation signal has appeared on the Net. It's on all the CommSats, the relay stations, and is being downloaded everywhere. The gold is coming!"

"Good," Mary said.

Cutter looked up at her. "I-I still don't see why we have

to do this. I mean, what's the bloody point? They say they're going to pay. We're going to get the damn gold. And that's the deal, isn't it? Isn't that what we want?"

"Shut up."

Mary came by Cutter and looked at the screen. What happened next had been planned. A computer station in Key West, a lone computer sitting in an empty rented room with an open link to the Net, sent out a message:

CONFIRMATION NOT RECEIVED IN TIME. PLEASE OBSERVE THE DEMONSTRATION.

"God—it isn't right," Cutter said. "They're going to pay us."

Mary imagined everyone seeing the message on their screens, the panic by all the fat cats in the resort, the confusion, the disorder.

"Hit it," Mary said.

Cutter, shaking his head, hit a key on the small computer pad . . .

Nathan Hale Bridger entered the *seaQuest*'s bridge and felt the tension. *Well,* he thought, *guess it's no surprise to the crew that our travel plans have been changed.*

He slid into his command chair—it still felt awkward—and immediately Ford was by his side.

"There's been a change in plans, Mr. Ford."

Bridger looked up at one of the VR screens above the helmsmen's chairs. "Set a new heading, one zero eight degrees, Mr. Ford. Thirty-degree starboard rudder, trim forward ballast."

"Aye, aye, Captain. We're taking her deep?" Ford seemed confused.

"I believe there's a nasty storm system growing in the direction we're heading, Mr. Ford, a real *El Niño.* I'd like us well below any turbulence. Another hundred meters down should do it."

Bridger watched the *seaQuest*'s helmsmen immediately carry out Ford's orders, and the giant sub smoothly responded.

Bridger looked over at Ortiz at the sensor station, with

Hitchcock standing beside him. "Lieutenant Hitchcock, are the WSKRS still deployed?"

"Yes, Captain. Do you want—"

"Bring in—what are they . . . Mother and Loner, but leave Junior swimming out there."

"Aye, aye, sir."

"And Ortiz, are we patched into the SousMer communications system?"

"Yes, Captain. I'm monitoring all their communications."

Ford turned away from the command chair, looking at a chart. "Oh—and, Mr. Ford, let's make it full speed ahead. Time may be a factor here."

"Aye, Captain."

Ortiz looked over from the sensor station and shouted. "Captain! There's been an explosion at SousMer!"

One of the VR screens suddenly displayed a schematic of SousMer, with a section flashing, showing damage.

Nobody said anything while the image of the resort floated on the screen, the damaged portion glowing red.

"So much for playing fair," Bridger said.

CHAPTER 5

The explosion made a funny muffled popping sound, Gooding thought. It sounded as if someone had had a giant plastic bag and gone *pop!* smashing their fist into it. But then the popping noise was followed by a long gust of smoke, and screaming—

And Gooding's nose twitched from the smell of burning plastic, melting cable. *A nasty smell . . .*

The alarm began ringing almost immediately, a high-pitched *thweep* that was accompanied by a pulsing red light to alert anyone unaware that something very bad had just happened.

The explosion must have been down near Communications, Harry Gooding thought. God, it may have even taken Communications out. But there were backup systems, redundancies. All you needed was a minicomputer with a cellular linkup.

Still, Gooding thought he'd best move in some other direction.

Which is when Sachio Kodei grabbed his shoulder.

Gooding stopped—he had no choice, the way Kodei held

43

him fast. Then he turned to face Kodei, who was wearing a headset.

"What—?" Gooding said.

"They want you to go outside. To take another look at your 'fish.' "

Gooding started shaking his head. There were limits to what one could do for the company. Besides, hadn't their TV host said that no one was to leave the resort? No minisubs sneaking away?

"I don't think I'd better," Gooding said. "I really don't think that's such a good idea. They may decide to blow the whole place up."

Kodei locked his other hand on Gooding's arm. "And so—if there's an explosive out there, we should leave it? Is that the idea?"

Then Kodei was distracted, nodding as someone chatted in his ear. "Yes," he said, speaking into the microphone, still not releasing Gooding. "He's going—"

And Kodei looked up at Gooding.

"Now."

Terry McShane looked at the desk with three VR monitors and keyboards. One SousMer employee sat at a keyboard, hitting the keys furiously.

Terry hurried to a chair next to him and pulled a free wireless keyboard close.

"Hey," the computer operator said. "What do you think you're doing?"

Terry looked at him. "Trying to save our butts," she said without missing a beat as her fingers hit the keyboard.

There would be no VR display, McShane knew. What appeared on the terminal would be gibberish, coded material that would mean nothing to the computer tech peering over her shoulder.

"What the heck are you doing?" he said. "I'll have to call Security."

Terry McShane paused in mid-stroke. "And my—aren't they doing a fine job." She gave the bewildered man a smile. "Better let me get this message off . . . to the UEO."

And that gave the man pause.

▲   ▲   ▲

Mary stood by her cabin door and listened.

The screaming outside stayed at a constant pitch—as the fat cats scrambled around, realizing that they were, in fact, trapped in a tin can at the bottom of the sea—a can that someone had just punched a hole in.

Well, not yet.

The exterior walls of SousMer weren't violated and would remain that way. The demonstration had merely brought down some of the engineering station and blown some smoke down the halls.

It was—all in all—a nice touch.

But the clock was running, and it was time to go.

Mary turned to Cutter, looking like a giant olive in his kelvar suit. The SousMer logo was prominently displayed, to silence any questions . . .

Cutter nodded glumly. The boy wanted out of here something fierce.

"Okay," Mary said, and she popped open the door and entered the mad party outside.

"Mr. Ford," Bridger said, watching the *seaQuest*'s progress on the center VR screen. The ship was running full-out now, near its top speed of 160 knots. "Do you have the course plotted . . . How long it will take?"

"Yes, Captain. We should be in the vicinity of SousMer by twenty-three hundred hours."

A little over three hours, Bridger thought. *seaQuest*'s speed was a wonder . . .

"Sir, should I sound battle stations before that—in case we meet some opposition?"

Bridger shook his head. "No. Get me Lucas. I want to talk with him . . . and start thinking about putting together an EVA team."

"Sir?" Ford said.

Bridger had hoped that his shakedown might have restored some of Ford's confidence. Judging by Ford's reaction, it didn't appear that it had.

"Mr. Ford—Admiral Noyce thinks that there's someone

still there. If we're lucky, he thinks we might catch them."

"And then, Captain—?"

Bridger grinned. "After that, I'm not too sure. But—"

"Captain." The voice was in Bridger's earpiece. He recognized Mundo Ortiz, his sensor chief. Bridger swiveled in the command chair and looked over at Ortiz at Communications.

"Sir, we have the tropical storm fully plotted. Would you like it displayed, Captain?"

"Yes," Bridger said. "On screen two— No, make that screen one." There was something reassuring about watching *seaQuest*'s steady progress through the water monitored by Junior swimming outside. The ship ran so smoothly, so silently, it was hard to believe that it was hustling at such phenomenal speed.

"Aye, aye, Captain," Ortiz said.

Despite everything, despite the danger to the people of SousMer, the potential danger to *seaQuest* herself, Bridger had to admit that, damn, he was enjoying this . . .

Geoffrey Harpe sat in his expansive office, dark, completely shaded against the afternoon sun. The blinds were drawn so he couldn't see his guests.

A party, he reminded himself . . . *I'm having a* party, *while halfway across the world* seaQuest DSV *is hurrying to protect my interests.*

I wonder how Nathan Hale Bridger feels about that.

I do hope, Harpe thought, *that Captain Bridger puts his heart and soul into the operation. There's more than bullion involved, there's people's lives and—God—the reputation of Harpe WorldWide.*

Let's not forget that.

And there was something else at risk . . .

There was a knock at the door. Michael Barrow, first in the Class of 2011 at Harvard Business, was at the door. His tanned face looked concerned.

"Yes, Michael?" Harpe said.

"Mr. Harpe—we have all the details of the pickup and delivery of the bullion."

Harpe nodded. There was no point in going back to the party. Not until this was over.

Harpe smiled. "Okay, Michael. I'll be right there. And would you make my apologies to my guests? Watch over everything . . . if you would."

"Of course, sir."

Harpe followed his assistant out, hating this as he did all situations that he couldn't totally control.

Dr. Richard Ernst stood up in the Seven Seas Lounge, looking around. *We're trapped,* he thought. How come there were no provisions for this kind of thing? Trapped by maniacs with explosives, and where the hell was the security?

Ernst reached out and poured himself another few fingers of Glenfiddich. Wonderfully, his fear was melting now under the warmth of the alcohol, transforming into anger. How the hell could the security here have been so damn lax?

They'd pay the money, Ernst knew that. He knew who the other guests were, the members of the British Parliament, the senators, the big shots from international business concerns, people who appeared every week in the news vids.

Of course, Ernst thought of his own work, where he was supposed to be going, the exciting breakthroughs that were happening. All of it very secret, revolutionary, and—perhaps—even frightening.

He was on the verge of being the most famous scientist of his time.

At thirty-two years old . . . it was incredible.

He took a big gulp of the scotch—

That is, if he didn't die here.

"Just move normally, steadily . . ." Mary looked over her shoulder at Cutter, the human olive, waddling behind her. So far, no staff members had questioned their moving from the first-floor suites down to the stairs leading to the sub pools.

Too much chaos to raise questions.

47

But then, looking ahead to the silvery doors to the pool, Mary saw trouble.

Two guards stood by the twin doors emblazoned with the rolling, wavy letters that spelled *SousMer*.

Mary stopped in front of them.

"Is everything okay here?" Mary said with what she knew sounded like authority.

One of the guards, a young kid, looked at the other. The other guard also looked confused. "Er, who sent you down here? What department are you—"

Mary shrugged, and then nodded. "Oh, right—" She reached into her case and pulled out, quickly, smoothly, the electron-mag stun gun.

She shot the older guard first, then the younger one, who was struggling to get out his gun. Each man was dead the instant the electrically charged dart hit him in the chest. Fast, painless . . . about as merciful a killing as you could want.

"Jeez," Cutter said.

"C'mon," Mary said. "Give me a hand dragging them inside."

Together, Mary and Cutter dragged the guards into the sub area, where—Mary feared—there might be more guards to be killed.

Though she guessed that most of Security was busy dealing with the pandemonium going on in the upper level of the resort—

Just as we planned it, she thought.

Gooding muttered to himself as he walked down the back staircase to the minisub pool.

This is a punishment, he thought. Plain and simple. *I screwed up—so my reward is getting sent out there.* Hadn't that guy said that they'd kill anyone who tried to leave? Well, they'd sure as hell kill anyone who tried to remove any of their explosives.

At least Gooding couldn't smell the smoke down here. The air smelled wet, salty—the smell of the pool filling the staircase. The metal stairs rattled as Gooding hurried.

Maybe if I do it fast, he thought. Get out there, look at the explosive, and get back in.

Do it fast, and maybe nothing would happen.

Gooding reached the back door to the sub area.

They wouldn't want him to remove the explosive. That would be suicide. It would go off, right? Taking Gooding and SousMer with it.

They couldn't want *that.*

Gooding hit a button and code on the keypad lock, and the metal door slid open.

And Gooding saw that he wasn't alone.

"That's amazing," Bridger said.

"Sir?" Ortiz said in his ear.

The storm had been named Mike, and Mike looked as if it was making a beeline for the party at SousMer.

"Chief," Bridger said to Ortiz, "what do I look at to get an idea of how big the storm is?"

"It's still growing, sir, but—"

Bridger watched the screen change, and now there was a series of graphs, each with three jagged lines filling it— red, yellow, blue.

"Red is the worst case, Captain. Blue is the best case. The range for error is actually pretty narrow. Satellite storm tracking doesn't make many mistakes."

One graph showed wind, another tidal factors accompanied by numbers. The meaning of any of it was not immediately apparent to Bridger.

"And it shows?"

"A very *big* tropical storm, Captain. A monster, if I might say."

There'd been some playing around with weather systems, Bridger knew—storm generation to bring water to the Sahara, trying to prevent mud slides in California, saving Russian crops.

But it only made things worse.

Bridger nodded. "But we're so far down it doesn't matter to us, right?"

"Yes, sir . . . and no."

49

Bridger saw Lucas standing next to him. "Commander Ford said you wanted me, Captain?" Bridger raised a hand to him, asking him to wait.

"Yes, Lucas—in a minute. Chief, you said 'yes and no' . . . I don't get it."

"Captain, SousMer is built on a volcanic shelf. It's perched on the same volcanic deposit that made the nearby island of St. Catherine. If the storm is big enough, there may be some very bad, very strange currents, tidal movement that, well, could reach down that deep."

"Nothing for us to worry about though, right—?"

Ortiz hesitated.

"Well, right, sir. I mean, pretty much. Can't bother the *seaQuest*. But—if you have to do any fast maneuvering down there, anything in the submersibles, any EVA activity, well, there are caves, caverns, all sorts of formations down there. It could get dicey."

Bridger nodded. *In other words,* he thought, *I do* have *to worry about this storm.*

"Thanks, Lieutenant." Bridger skipped off his headset and got out of his command chair.

"Lucas, I'd like a private chat with you—and Darwin."

Bridger led the *seaQuest*'s young computer whiz back to the dolphin tank, where, Bridger thought, Darwin seemed to be waiting for them . . .

Gooding stood at the other end of the sub pool. He saw two people dressed in odd suits dragging something—no, *someone* to the side.

Now, what is this? Gooding thought.

And when he imagined that he should take that question to his boss *prontissimo,* one of the figures, slender, almost . . . feminine . . .

She looked over and—dropping the body she was dragging—said:

"Don't even think of moving."

Gooding saw that the woman was holding something in her hand. He wondered how much worse this day could get, while he did exactly what the woman ordered.

CHAPTER 6

Mary looked at the man standing at the other end of the sub pool. Some of the two-person subs were still wet from their last trip outside the resort only hours ago.

A larger transport sub floated to the right, designed to ferry guests from St. Cats to the resort. Two other subs, clunky deep-ocean submersibles, shiny ball bearings with arms, dangled from giant hoists.

"That's it—don't move," Mary said.

"What the bloody hell is he doing here?" Cutter said.

"Relax. Everything's fine. Get your computer running so we know what's happening."

Mary turned back to the SousMer employee standing by the rear door. "Now, I want you to come over here. That's it—very slowly, with your arms at your sides."

"Are you going to kill him?" Cutter whispered. He had perched the computer on the bench where the guests removed their diving suits.

"Shut up," Mary whispered back.

The man kept walking toward them, a glum expression on his face.

Killing him was a possibility—but too risky. The man

had probably been sent down here, and if he simply disappeared, more people would come down here. Things could get messy . . .

"That's it," Mary said, her gun aimed at Gooding's chest. *I don't want to kill him,* Mary thought. *Not yet, anyway.*

Then the man was in front of her. She read his name, embroidered on the lapel of his navy blue shirt.

H. Gooding.

"Well, H. Gooding . . . can you tell us what you're doing down here?"

She watched his eyes flicker down to the body on the floor, then to Cutter playing with his computer.

"There's still a problem with the computer," Cutter said breathlessly. "Maybe we're down too deep, but—"

Mary didn't turn to Cutter, but she said, "*Now* you have a problem. We need that computer link." She shifted the gun to her other hand, fatigued from holding it up, keeping it pointed at H. Gooding. "If there's a problem, solve it."

She turned her attention back to Gooding.

"So now—what are we going to do with you?"

It's funny Terry McShane thought as she sat in front of the computer screen. *Funny that I happened to be here . . . for a completely different reason . . . when the resort became hostage.*

Though she wasn't too sure what good she could do down here. She was only another hostage.

The screen flashed a coded sequence of letters, which Terry stared at for a moment before mentally using the cipher based on a key word, translating the line of letters to read, MESSAGE RECEIVED. INSTRUCTIONS TO FOLLOW.

Key-word ciphers were easy to crack—if you had the key word. In this cipher, each line of text used a different key word to scramble the alphabet . . . and the sequence of key words was based on a passage memorized by all level three intelligence officers at the UEO.

It was a quick and easy way to get some security—when any system's ICE could be cracked. Not exactly a high-tech code, it meant that any terminal, anywhere, could be used

52

with a reasonable assurance of security. If anyone were monitoring this conversation, it would take them hours to unscramble all the lines.

The computer tech next to McShane turned to her.

"Miss, I don't know who you are. And I don't know what you're doing. But you can't use this terminal. I gotta call Security."

McShane smiled and dug into a small pocket in the back of her skirt. She dug out a white card.

"Go ahead," McShane said. "Strip it."

The tech took the card and pulled it through the magnetic reader on the console. The screen blinked, announced that it was "searching"—and then it flashed Terry's face, name, and the information that she was with the UEO, Information and Research Division—immediate supervisor, Admiral William Noyce.

The technician nodded. "Okay—I guess you're cleared."

But Terry had her eyes on the screen in front of her, looking at another line of code, a long one this time. McShane mentally inserted the key word at the beginning of the alphabet, then filled in the other letters, ready to decode each word.

Stay . . . in . . . contact . . . DSV—

Her breath caught. She knew what was coming, and the surprise, and her feelings, caught her like an icy breeze, chilling her . . .

seaQuest DSV *is proceeding to location. Stand by.*

seaQuest. McShane had heard about the change in command, about the new captain. Someone had told her at UEO headquarters before she grabbed the transcontinental shuttle for the East Coast.

"Yes," a friend had said, "didn't you hear? They got Nathan Bridger to take command."

And then—

"Hey, didn't you know him, years ago? Didn't you work with him?"

Nodding, turning away, because time can make some things better, and it can make other things go away. But not Bridger. He was a memory that wouldn't go away.

And now—life can be so strange—here was Bridger cruising to this resort, the cavalry rushing to the fort.

Terry turned to the computer operator. "Now tell me—where can I find the director?"

Bridger led Lucas over to the dolphin tank aft of the bridge. Darwin swerved back and forth.

"Want to . . . play?" his synthesized voice chirped through the speaker.

Bridger shook his head. "Not now, Darwin."

There was a clipping sound. "A problem?"

Bridger nodded. "Yes. And I need your help."

Darwin splashed in the water, excited.

"He's ready," Lucas said. "How can I help, Captain?"

"You said something about 'modifications' before, that you made modifications to Darwin's speech program linking him to the ship. What exactly are they?"

Lucas took his Marlins hat and turned it brim forward. "I only helped with the programming. It was Ortiz's idea . . ."

"Go on."

Lucas leaned closer to Bridger. *Was this some kind of secret?* Bridger thought. *And—shouldn't they have gotten my permission?* After all, he was the captain.

"We thought—wouldn't it be great if Darwin could access *seaQuest*'s systems directly."

"Directly? What do you mean?"

"Get information directly from the ship's systems, through the same chip that turns his dolphin talk into words. So—that's what we did."

Bridger turned and looked at Darwin.

"Problems . . . ," Darwin said. "Storm . . . explosives . . . you have *big* problem."

Bridger grinned.

Lucas leaned close to the tank. "He can get the information as soon as you can, Captain. Maybe faster. I hope you don't mind, but now it's like he has a computer in his head."

And sure, Darwin still *looked* happy—though Bridger

worried that it might all be too much for Darwin. He was a smart mammal, no mistaking that. But was he adapted to deal with this flood of information?

The thing Darwin liked best was to play.

Or so Bridger thought.

"Okay. We'll try it out, see how Darwin does with it."

The dolphin splashed in the water, slapping the surface with his tail. There was a time, Bridger thought, when that was all the communicating that the animal could do.

"I . . . help problem?"

"I hope so, Darwin." Bridger turned back to Lucas. "You know where we're going? You know what's happened?"

Lucas nodded, his face serious.

"I have an idea," Bridger said. "It involves Darwin. And I want you to tell me whether it's possible."

Darwin came close to the thick Plexiglas to be part of the huddle . . .

"There. I've got it. There must have been some interference from the electronics down here, all the subs . . ." Cutter aimed the holographic image from his computer console into a point in the air a few feet away.

"Good. Now," Mary said, looking at Harry Gooding. She had asked him his name, and now she used it. "Harry, we want to use one of these subs you have here to get out. Now, why don't you tell us what *you're* supposed to be doing down here?"

"I-I was supposed to go outside."

Mary nodded, waiting, the gun only feet away from Gooding, who was sweating despite the chill from the cool ocean water.

"And what were you supposed to *do* outside, Harry?"

"I had seen something. On one of the power plants. On my last inspection. I thought it was a fish—"

Mary turned to Cutter. "I told you. God, they spotted it."

"So," Cutter said, "it's not as if they can get it off."

Back to Gooding, Mary smiled. "And you were going to take another look?"

Gooding nodded. "And—and, if it looked like an explosive, I guess they'd want me to try and get it off—"

"Good bloody thing you didn't get near it," Cutter said. "Would have blown us all sky high. Hey, what's this—what the bloody—"

The holographic screen floating in the pool area was displaying a screen from a specialized program tracking all the communications in and out of the resort. Rafael didn't want any surprises.

"What," Cutter said, "is *this*?"

Mary looked at the data, the numbers, the floating windows telling Cutter that someone was communicating in the station.

"What is it? What's wrong?" she said.

"Someone has set up a direct link out of the resort. I'm not sure—but it looks like they're using the same ultra high-band frequency used by the UEO."

"So, they're talking, reassuring each other, telling themselves that everything's going to be—"

"No. This stuff, this traffic is all in some kind of code . . ."

"So break it—"

Cutter shook his head. "It's changing . . . each line, a different pattern. Looks like a substitution cipher. Antiquated stuff. Yeah, that's what it is. No voice, only alphanumeric stuff. Changing every bloody line."

"*Break* it, I said."

Cutter laughed. "Sure. But it will take a while to crack the first line, then another bit for the second line, and on and on. In the meantime we won't know what's happening."

Mary turned back to Gooding.

"You've come at very useful time, Harry. They'll be looking for you to leave in a sub . . . to check things out. They'll be waiting for *you* to leave."

Gooding nodded.

Mary smiled. "It's all very convenient."

"I don't know," Lucas said. "I can try."

Bridger nodded. He was no systems expert. It was up

to Lucas to tell him whether his plan would work or not. And—so far—it looked as if the kid wasn't intimidated.

"I . . . try *too*," Darwin said.

"Good work, now if—"

"Captain!" Lieutenant Bachmann called to Bridger from the communications station.

Bridger turned back to Lucas. "Go to it, Lucas."

"Yes, sir." And Lucas hurried away, while Bridger walked over to Bachmann's communications console.

"Captain, I've got something coming in from the UEO." Bridger put on his earpiece. "Which screen, Lieutenant?"

"Screen one, sir."

Bridger nodded, then the data screens disappeared and Admiral Noyce was there.

"Nathan, we have completed our search and scan of the guests of SousMer. And we think we've got something."

"Go ahead head, Admiral . . . I'm watching."

Noyce disappeared, and there was a photo of a woman, and a name—*Mary Knox*. She was an attractive blonde, but the woman's face was drawn, sullen. The name meant nothing to Bridger.

"Mary Knox, aka Mary Bristol, aka Samantha Cronin, aka Bloody Mary . . . Knox is connected to over thirty acts of piracy and terrorism, including the raid on the Bounty Trough Mining Colony, off New Zealand."

That was an incident Nathan had heard about. Forty people were killed when a trio of modified Skipjacks and Tridents raided the colony and made off with tons of pure sulfides and rare ore deposits.

It was a brutal, vicious raid. Rafael Vargas was blamed—it had all his hallmarks—and he didn't deny his involvement. The sick thing was that there had been no reason to kill anyone.

"Mary Knox is considered Rafael Vargas's second in command."

Then there was another face, a pudgy fellow with dark eyes, perpetually guilty.

The name below the photo read, *John Cutter.*

"Jack Cutter once worked for Harpe Enterprises' Deep-Sea Mining Division. He is an explosives expert, best in the business. When Harpe discovered he was selling black-market organic explosives to the combines, he was arrested, but later Cutter was sprung in an action that showed the marks of Rafael. All the guards were killed, the other prisoners on the transport to the penal island were killed . . . only Cutter was taken."

Right, Bridger thought. That's one way to buy employee loyalty.

Now Bridger waited for the bad news he was sure would come.

Noyce cleared his throat. "Nathan, it appears that both Knox and Cutter entered the resort without a ripple from SousMer security."

Maybe things will get tighter after this, Bridger thought. Lock that barn door.

"And Nathan—we think that they're still there."

Sure, that made sense. They couldn't risk having explosives discovered. It had to be done fast. Plant them, and then get away, making sure no one was around to watch the escape.

"So, we may be able to do something—"

Not, thought Bridger, if everything they said was carried on the Net. It was time to cut Noyce out of the loop. If anything was going to be done, it would be done without sending every message up to the Net.

"Admiral, I have taken steps to deal with the situation."

Noyce's face looked confused.

"Nate—the bullion is in the air. We don't want to do anything to jeopardize rescuing the hostages—"

"Yes, sir. And therefore I'd like to recommend that any communications with the resort go directly through *seaQuest*."

Bridger looked over at Bachmann, who wore a surprised smile on learning that he had just become Hostage Central.

Come on, Nathan thought, read between the lines here. Those people in SousMer were dead whether or not Rafael

58

got his bullion. Unless they could save them . . . some-how . . .

Bill Noyce, who knew Bridger all too well, nodded. After all, hadn't Noyce brought ice cream to the island . . . pulling Bridger back from the peace, the serenity of his work . . . to this?

"Right, Captain, that's a good idea." Noyce started to turn away . . .

"And, Nathan—good luck."

Noyce disappeared from the screen. Bridger walked over to his command chair. Ford came over to him from Navigation.

"Captain, we'll be in the area in about twenty minutes. Do you want to order battle stations and ready the plasma torpedoes?"

"No, Mr. Ford. Just tell me who's on that EVA team I requested."

Ford grinned. "Weapons Officer Phillips, sir. He's trained with explosives."

"And the second man?"

"Oh—and myself, sir."

CHAPTER 7

Cutter looked up. "I've cracked the first line. Someone inside is talking to the UEO. See—"

Mary looked at the message floating in the air. So what? What could the UEO do with such little time? The clock was running and the gold was in the air.

She turned to Harry Gooding.

"Here's what we're going to do, Harry. We'll take one of your subs out and *you'll* drive—"

Cutter interrupted. "You think that's such a good idea? What if—"

"It's a great bloody idea." Then, back to Gooding, "You know what they'll want to hear, Harry, what they'll be waiting for. And—at some point—you'll lose communications and get us the hell out of here."

At which point, she thought, Harry Gooding would be dead. And after the terrible resort tragedy, she'd make her way to St. Cat's western side, where, after a night swim, she and Cutter would end up on the rocky coast . . . only a little wet for their trouble.

"Do you understand?"

Gooding nodded.

Such a clever lad.

"So then, let's get the sub ready. Which one shall we take?"

Gooding pointed at a dark green maintenance sub docked to one side off the large moon pool.

"That's my regular maintenance submersible. That's the one I usually take."

"Good. Then, what are we waiting for?" Mary turned to Cutter. "Close down shop, Jack. We're leaving the party."

But Cutter shook his head, looking at the hard VR screen of his computer.

"Wait a minute. Wait—check this out. I've cracked another line of the code. Oh, God, this ain't—"

"What is it? What's the problem?"

When Mary turned to the holographic screen image, her eyes saw only one word.

seaQuest . . .

Bridger shook his head. "No. I appreciate the offer, Commander, but I need you here, Mr. Ford. Find someone else—"

"Captain, EVA is one of my responsibilities, sir. It's what I'm supposed to do."

Bridger smiled. "Not this kind of EVA, Mr. Ford. I'm sure that you can—"

"Sir—"

Bridger stopped. There was a tone in Ford's voice that was just this side of disobedience. Bridger turned back to his exec. Then Ford lowered his voice a bit.

A good thing because, damn it, Bridger saw that the entire bridge was watching this scene. *Is this a test of my leadership? That's something I don't need,* he thought.

"Captain—I'd like to request a private word with you."

Bridger kept looking at Ford. It couldn't have been easy for Ford to turn over *seaQuest.* How much resentment did he have?

Bridger nodded. "Fine, Mr. Ford. Head to my quarters— I'll be right there."

Ford nodded, and Bridger got out of the command chair, thinking over the possibilities. Everyone was watching him, evaluating him. "Lieutenant Bachmann," Bridger said to his communications officer, "are we linked with the resort?"

"Yes, Captain. And someone inside is trying to communicate with us via an alphanumeric code."

"Probably knows that someone inside is listening. Can you read it?"

"No problem, sir. It's a UEO key-word cipher. I'll have it up for you in a minute . . ."

Then Bridger felt someone touch his shoulder.

"Nathan . . ." Bridger turned around to see Matt Crocker standing next to him. And Chief of the Helm Crocker's normally smiling face looked troubled.

"What is it, Gator? How bad am I screwing this up?"

Crocker shook his head. He spoke quietly. "That's not for me to say, Nathan. But you do know that crew on the bridge are watching how this goes down."

Bridger cleared his throat. "I can see that."

"So, what are you going to do?"

"I don't want to send my exec out on what may be a suicide mission—"

"It's his responsibility, Nathan."

"And this ship is mine."

Crocker shook his head. "You still having trouble taking advice, eh?"

Bridger smiled. "Excuse me, I've got a meeting." The Captain took a few steps and then stopped and turned. "It's comforting, isn't it, Gator, that some things never change?"

Harpe paced in the small communications room of his Hawaiian beach complex.

"There's nothing more coming from the UEO, Mr. Harpe."

"And from SousMer?"

The communications tech shook her head. "No, sir. Nothing is going out on the Net, though the frequency scanners are picking up coded traffic between the resort and another party—which is approaching the resort."

Harpe nodded. Another party . . . *seaQuest*. And what would *seaQuest* do?

Well, that was obvious, Harpe could figure that out.

Noyce thought that they were going to blow the place up anyway, and he wanted Bridger to stop it.

So—where does that leave me? Harpe thought. *Me and the hundred million in bullion that I'm about to drop in the Pacific Ocean?*

It leaves me throwing good money after bad.

"Get me the transport," Harpe said.

"Sir?"

"Patch me through to the C-137. I've changed my mind."

The door to Bridger's stateroom clicked closed.

"Okay, Commander. Let's hear it."

"EVAs are my responsibility, sir. All EVAs, and especially one this important. If anyone should do it, it should be me."

"Even something as crazy as this, Mr. Ford?"

"*Especially* something as crazy as this, Captain."

"It's too dangerous—"

"Captain," Ford interrupted and Bridger looked up. There was a fine line Ford was walking here . . . "Captain, do you know what it was like, growing up in Chicago during the gang wars? I lost a brother. My best friend got shot walking down the street, and he was doing nothing."

"I know—it was bad, Commander."

"No. You *don't* know how bad it was, sir. It was a war zone. The TV crews didn't get in, and the newspapers printed what Washington told them. But for people trapped in the city, for the kids, it was their Stalingrad, their Tet Offensive. And if I lived, it was because I swore that things would change, could change."

Bridger rubbed his chin.

Ford took a step closer to his commanding officer. "And a gang is a gang, sir. In Chicago or down here. I didn't back down then, I didn't run then. I don't want to start now. I have my job to do."

Ford took a breath.

"Let me do it."

Bridger laughed. "You know, that's precisely the decision I just came to, Commander. Now, get Weapons Officer Phillips and we'll meet at the moon pool. If you're so eager to do this, let's get started. Who knows how much time we have . . ."

"The submersible can hold three people? Looks small . . . ," the man, the one called Cutter, said, peering into the hatch of the minisub.

Gooding cleared his throat. "It's a tight squeeze, but we'll fit."

The woman seemed unconcerned. "What's the procedure? How do you get out?"

"The pool doors to the outside are closed until I request permission for them to open."

The woman turned to Cutter. "And you can monitor his request?" Then, back to Gooding, "Not that you'd try anything, right, Harry?"

"Yes—no problem," Cutter said.

"If the *seaQuest* is outside, we're going to have to set off another charge, just to warn them away."

"The one in the air shaft will work nicely."

"We'll be listening to what you say, Gooding. So make sure everything sounds exactly the way it's supposed to."

Gooding nodded.

"Let's go then," the woman said.

Bridger hurried off the elevator from the bridge and saw that Lucas, Hitchcock, and Darwin—splashing around in the water—were gathered by the sub pool.

Ford and Phillips were already in their EVA suits. Their heads—still without the massive helmets that acted as gills—were dwarfed by the bulky suits. And though the suits looked cumbersome, Bridger knew that they were amazingly flexible.

Buoyancy could be adjusted, and a small propulsion system could be used to travel short distances underwater . . .

almost like moon walking, hopping through the water in slow motion, able to make graceful leaps.

Someday, thought Bridger, *I'd like to try one of those suits . . .*

"You've told them what to expect?" he said to Lucas.

Lucas nodded.

"Lucas told me too." Darwin's voice was carried on the moon pool's loudspeaker.

Bridger came over to the pool and touched the water, and then rubbed his wet hand affectionately over the beaklike nose of Darwin.

"You too, pal. So—where do we stand, Lucas?"

"Everything's crystal, Captain. According to the plans I downloaded from the UEO, SousMer has three emergency entrances. Lieutenant Phillips and Commander Ford will use one to gain entrance—"

"And what will keep our friends inside from not picking that up?"

"Well, that's where I come in. While they're out there, I'm going to crack the SousMer system and override its warning system."

"You can do that?"

"Sure," Lucas groaned. "At least, I think so."

"Sounds way too risky to me," Katherine Hitchcock said. "Could make them set the whole place off. And we're not even sure they're still in there."

"They're still there, count on it," Bridger said. "But once they're out, they'd have us over a barrel. Come near the resort, and it's history. Our only hope is that they don't want to commit suicide."

Bridger looked at Hitchcock. "Ford and Phillips should be able to get in through the emergency exits?"

"They should. I checked the engineering of the place, and those doors are designed for someone in trouble, a worker outside the resort. But—well, I can't guarantee that our friends won't know that we're coming in."

Bridger turned to Lucas. "That's your job."

"I'm sure I can crack the system, get to the command programs." Lucas nodded. "Should be no problem."

Bridger hoped that Lucas was as competent as he seemed confident. Then he turned to Darwin.

"Darwin, you know what you have to do?"

The dolphin used his tail fin to rise out of the water. It was a familiar joyful action by the dolphin.

The words still took some getting used to . . .

"I get explosive off—"

Lieutenant Hitchcock touched Bridger's shoulder. "We figure Darwin will have eight, ten seconds *tops*. After that, it will blow, Captain."

Bridger tried to imagine those seconds ticking off, Darwin moving through the water. He wished that there were another, better alternative.

Of course, the only alternative was playing roulette with six hundred lives.

"I guess that's it, then—"

A screen above the pool shifted. Ortiz's face appeared. "Captain, I have a topo of the area surrounding SousMer."

The VR screen filled with a three-dimensional model of the seafloor near the resort. "Bridger to Helm," the Captain said. "Gator, you there? Can you see this?"

"Yes, Captain."

Bridger waited a second while the image rotated. "Hold it right there, Ortiz. Right, Gator, let's try to hide the *seaQuest* right behind that escarpment, put her about one klick from the resort."

"As if they won't know we're here," Hitchcock said.

"But as far as they're concerned, we're just observing."

"Aye, Captain."

Bridger nodded to Ford and Phillips. "Gentlemen, it's time to go swimming."

Gooding turned switches, flipping them one at a time.

"God—can't you hurry?" Mary said.

Gooding shook his head. "I have to make sure all systems are clear. It's not a little underwater jet speeder."

"Okay, okay—Cutter, what's going on outside?"

"Damn, the sub's right out there."

"And it's still coming?"

"No—the *seaQuest* has stopped." Cutter looked up to her. "About a kilometer away. But I don't like this."

"Don't worry. The sub will stay there as long as it thinks that the people are in danger." Mary laughed. "Maybe we'll get lucky and the *seaQuest* will come close and we can get two birds with one stone."

"I don't think Bridger would be that stupid . . . ," Cutter said quietly.

"What? What was that?"

"Er—I said I don't think Bridger would be that stupid."

Right, Mary thought. Nathan Bridger was now captain of the *seaQuest*. Lured out of mourning. He was smart . . . surely he'd be cautious with so many lives.

A whirring noise started inside the submersible, and then a louder hum from the rear.

"We can get going now," Gooding said.

"Get in," Mary ordered Cutter, who closed the cover of his computer. Then, with one last look around the doomed resort, "Let's blow this firetrap."

The director of SousMer, Jacques Farrand, stood behind Terry McShane, rubbing his knuckles nervously. Poor man, she thought. For someone with a job description that probably stressed social skills, this was an unfortunate turn of events.

"I must admit, Ms. McShane, that I am a bit worried that you are in contact with this sub, this *seaQuest*."

"This sub, this *seaQuest,* is the only thing that may save everyone's life here, Monsieur Farrand."

"Oh, no—the bullion is being delivered. There will be no"—Terry wanted to laugh—"problems."

Terry stood quietly and waited for *seaQuest*'s contact—not having a clue what Bridger had planned.

Still at the moon pool, Bridger looked up at the VR screens and saw the view from both Phillips's and Ford's headgear. The two men were walking down steps into the pool. A small exit compartment was at the end of the pool.

"All set, gentlemen?"

"Everything's fine, Captain," Ford answered through the intercom.

Bridger turned and watched Hitchcock finish strapping Darwin into his own "suit," the communications rig that would travel with him, allowing two-way communications while he swam to the resort.

"Darwin, can you hear me?"

"I hear . . . *great!*"

Bridger looked at Lucas. "You'd better get to your keyboard, Lucas. I'm going back on the bridge." Bridger started for the elevator chute.

"Captain—"

It was Ortiz's voice over the speaker. "WSKRS data on SousMer is starting to come in. I'm analyzing it for explosives."

"I'll be right up, Mr. Ortiz." And the Captain hurried back up to the command center of his ship.

The hatch to the maintenance sub slammed shut and then automatically locked.

"We can go?" Mary said.

"Yes. I should check in with Communications. Let them know I'm leaving."

Mary nodded. "Go ahead then."

She watched Gooding adjust his headset. Mary wore a similar pair, monitoring everything he said.

"Harry Gooding here, and I'm ready to take a look outside. Please open the western sub gate."

Harry waited.

"Just a minute, Gooding." Harry recognized the voice of Sachio Kodei. "Just a minute, please."

Gooding looked at Mary, and smiled nervously . . .

CHAPTER 8

Bridger sat in his command chair. The three VR screens dead ahead showed the dark images from Ford's and Phillips's headsets, a WSKRS scan of the resort, and information coming in from the Net.

The lights from the EVA team's headsets picked up the tiny particles of food and plankton drifting to the seafloor, a steady rain of material. One screen picked up a stingray startled by the divers. It glided away, flying underwater and showing its cloud-white underside.

"The tropical storm is due here in about two hours, Captain."

"Ortiz, any word on what effects—if any—we'll get down here?"

"Hard to tell, sir. But the way the resort is perched, on a bit of island shelf, sir, it could catch some currents. Might get turbulent for the EVA team."

"Commander Ford, do you copy that?"

Bridger watched the image caught by the microcamera in Ford's helmet. By a combination of leaping and tiny thrusts from the EVA suits' propulsion units, Ford and Phillips were climbing up a small underwater ridge.

"We copy, sir."

They couldn't see the resort yet.

"Ortiz—what has WSKRS picked up?"

"Just this, Captain—check screen two."

Bridger leaned forward in his chair. The probe had circled the resort, a small silent spy—hopefully undetected by anyone inside.

"I don't see anything." The resort's lights glowed eerily in the dark water.

Place looked damned gloomy . . .

"Captain, here it is." The image of the resort changed, as Junior swung under a large spherical wing. "That's the main power and life-support plant. And—there!"

Bridger saw it—something stuck to the underbelly of the plant.

"Analysis?"

"Coming up, Captain. Same screen."

The resort disappeared, and there was a schematic of the disk-shaped object. It was, the information on the screen reported, a bio-explosive, one of the new generation of explosive materials that could not be detected by scanners. It would be read as organic material. Wear it close to your gut like a heating pad, and nobody would pick it up.

"Sir—there's also this."

A small chip appeared on the screen. "That's the detonator, sir. A small CPU in constant communication with whoever's got their finger on the button."

This explained how they'd gotten the stuff onto the resort.

"Lieutenant Bachmann—can you send this down to Lucas?"

But Wolenczak's voice was already in Bridger's ear.

"I'm getting the feed along with you, sir."

"And Darwin too?" Bridger said.

Bridger waited . . . and then he heard Darwin's electronic voice, growing ever more familiar.

"Yes—I see it!" Darwin said.

"Careful, Darwin," Bridger said.

Lucas's voice again. "I'm sending all the data right to Darwin, sir."

"How about getting into the SousMer computer, Mr. Wolenczak? You said that it would be—"

"No problem, sir. It's just that I'm hitting some ICE now, but nothing I can't handle."

The kid was nothing if not modest, Bridger thought.

"I don't want any alarms going off when the EVA team goes in."

"Don't worry, sir. I'm on the case. Don't worry."

Advice that Bridger ignored.

"What's the problem?" Mary said, poking Gooding.

"I'm waiting for clearance to leave."

"I don't like this," Cutter said.

"We're leaving. Get the sub moving," she ordered Gooding.

For a moment he didn't move. He sat there, sweating even more, frozen. Mary jabbed him with her gun.

"Now, I said—"

Gooding grabbed the stick of the sub. Mary saw that he pressed a button and the engine hummed. The stick he held looked as if it controlled the flaps on the sides. She felt the sub tilt downward.

I could fly this . . . she thought. *Can't be any harder than piloting a Skipjack.*

"Something's up," Cutter said. "I don't like it."

He really does chatter too much, Mary thought. *There's got to be a solution for that . . . when this is over.*

"Sit back and enjoy the ride, Mr. Cutter."

"What's this?" Terry McShane said to Farrand, pointing at a blip on her screen.

"One of the subs is moving, a maintenance man."

"But you told him to wait."

The SousMer director shrugged. "Perhaps he misunderstood."

Then there was another message, an intrusion alert, on the screen. Someone trying to enter the computer system.

The ICE's early warning system automatically kicked in. First, McShane thought it might be the terrorists, trying to make the system crash. But then—

The technician leaned over to her. "The sub, *seaQuest,* is linked up. And—boy—someone's working very hard to get into our system."

"Can you let them? Let them take over," Terry said.

"I can't disable all the systems. Not fast enough, anyway. But it doesn't matter—they're doing fine on their own . . ."

Ford stood next to Phillips on a rocky ledge made up of volcanic debris, probably hundreds of thousands of years old, he guessed. It was stuff left over from when the island chain was made.

Phillips pointed at the resort and made a gesture—*There it is.* It looked like a Christmas tree, lights flickering, seen through black sheets.

They were observing radio silence. *seaQuest* could pick up their video images, but there was to be no voice, nothing to indicate that they were going to try and get into the resort.

Ford waited a second, and then he pressed the small thrusters at the sides of his EVA suit. He glided off the volcanic mound, a gentle leap toward the seafloor . . . and SousMer.

Darwin swam by the explosive. Looking at it, wondering about it.

Bridger now watched the dolphin through the eyes of Junior, hovering a hundred meters away.

"That's it, Dar. Just hang in there. Wait for our signal."

Eight . . . ten seconds. That's what Hitchcock figured. That's all the time Darwin would have. It didn't seem like much.

It's funny, Bridger thought, so much power in this ship— but everything was happening *out there.*

Terry stood up. Something was up with that minisub.

"Get some of your security people, Monsieur Farrand.

Can you keep access to the outside closed?"

"You mean, stop the sub? Well, yes, but Gooding is simply carrying out—"

"Then do it—"

McShane stood up. "And get everyone as close to the center of the resort as possible."

There could be another demonstration of how serious the terrorists were.

Ford watched Phillips jump ahead a bit, his jet-assisted leaps landing him only meters away from the surface of the resort.

Then Phillips was right there, touching the emergency door handle. Hitchcock had told them that she didn't have a clue how it worked—those specs weren't available. But it seemed to work on a compression system.

Pull the lever and a chamber on the other side opened to the sea.

If it worked.

And if Lucas could cover their tracks.

Ford made two short jumps to get close to the door. His landing sent up a smoky spray of seafloor sand. Phillips looked over at Ford—and the executive officer nodded . . . and watched Phillips pull on the handle.

Gooding piloted the sub smoothly toward the opening to the sea. The minisub's lights picked up the shiny silver walls of the chamber leaving the pool.

Then he saw that the launch gates were closed.

"They're closed," he said. "I don't know—"

The woman pressed her gun into his ribs. "What?"

"They're not letting us out."

"I knew this would happen," Cutter said.

"Shut up." Then the woman turned to Gooding. "Speak to them. Tell them you're ready to go outside. Tell them to open the doors."

Gooding turned on his radio.

"Er, Harry Gooding here. I'm ready to go outside. Please open—"

Gooding heard the tension in Kodei's voice. "Harry—come on back."

Gooding nodded. He looked up at the woman, searching for what her next move was.

She appeared stymied, looking around the cramped quarters of the sub, shaking her head. Then—

"Is there another way to get that damn gate open?"

"B-back at the sub pool. There's a control station. It's designed for emergencies, computer failure. Things like that. We could do it there."

"Okay—bring the sub back up, Harry. And then we'll show everyone why they'd better let us go."

Gooding, wishing he didn't feel so trapped, so scared, turned the sub around.

The storm curled past the thin continental shelf off eastern South America, picking up moisture and tremendous wind speed, until it finally became a full-blown tropical storm, a big one, an *El Niño* . . .

The UEO weather service had named it Mike.

Mike passed over an island named, whimsically enough, Hell, and summarily flattened expensive hotels and shacks with equal impunity.

Now, still growing stronger, it continued north, relentlessly heading toward St. Cat—

CHAPTER 9

Bridger leaned forward in the command chair.

On one of the VR screens, he saw the elegantly curved exterior wall of SousMer, and Phillips's hand yanking down hard on the emergency handle.

Nothing was happening.

"Hitchcock," Bridger said to his engineer, standing next to him, "what's the problem?"

"Captain—I don't know. It should open. Unless there's some kind of internal lock. Could be that—"

"Great. And they're stuck out there knocking on the door."

"Are you going to have them try another—"

And then—on the screen—there was movement. The panel in the side of the underwater complex opened, and Phillips turned and gave a thumbs-up sign at Ford.

"Lieutenant Bachmann—tell Darwin to stand by. God, things are going to happen fast now."

Ford pulled himself into the interior chamber after Phillips, and he wondered what kind of alarms were going off now—

or if Lucas had already cracked the security system, masking their entrance.

Come on, Lucas, he thought. *Be as good as you say you are.*

The chamber had ladders inside that led from the opening up into the water-filled compartment. Ford climbed quickly, taking the metal steps two at a time. Phillips, right behind him, pointed ahead, at another handle and buttons at the other end.

Yes, that must be it, Ford figured. That handle must be the way to shut the panel, drain the water, and get some air inside.

Ford reached the handle and gave it a quick yank—and suddenly he heard the sound of the panel closing again and water being sucked out. The water moved fast, but still they had to wait until the room was only dripping.

Then Ford hit another button—and the entrance to SousMer opened.

They were staring at two people who had electron-mag guns pointed right at them.

Darwin kept swimming back and forth, looking at the curious thing. And he could picture what it would do, the brilliant explosion, the fire—the pain. He could understand *that.*

It didn't look like anything bad . . . but Darwin knew what it could do.

So Darwin tried very hard not to think about that.

The small submersible broke the surface of the pool. Mary looked through the glass and once again saw the shiny metal of the sub pool's walls.

"Okay," she said to Gooding. "Go wherever you have to fast and get the gate open." She turned to Cutter. "What's going on inside?"

"No communications, nothing in code at least, nothing leaving the resort."

"Then why the hell are they screwing with us?"

The sub moved slowly, gliding close to one of the bays. "Can't you go any faster?"

"I-I'm trying to dock it," Gooding said.

Mary looked at her watch. The gold bullion should be somewhere over the Pacific, heading toward the drop site. And time had almost run out for SousMer.

Which means . . . that time has almost run out for us, Mary thought.

"Move it," she whispered. "Move it . . ."

On the screens, Bridger saw the guns aimed at Ford and Phillips.

Crocker watched beside him. "Quite a welcome they're getting, eh, Captain?"

"Lucas," Bridger said into his microphone. "Lucas, are you into the computer yet?"

"Not completely, sir. It has some wicked ICE, especially around its security programs. In a few minutes I should have access to everything."

Bridger looked over at Bachmann. "Can we risk voice contact?"

"It might be picked up, sir."

Bridger shook his head.

"Okay . . . okay, I'll wait—and see what happens."

And that's when Bridger saw Terry McShane. Short auburn hair, green eyes, a face from his past—and for a minute he was speechless.

McShane spoke to the two divers.

Most likely they were from *seaQuest,* but she had to be sure.

"Okay, could you two stand over there, against the wall?"

The two men didn't move, and McShane realized that they couldn't hear her through their helmets. She made a gesture for them to remove them. *It's okay,* she signaled. She saw the *seaQuest* logo on their suits.

So this *is* the cavalry . . .

The two men removed their helmets and McShane half-expected to see Nathan Bridger in the flesh.

One helmet came off, and a handsome African-American smiled at her. "We're from the *seaQuest.*" He stuck out his hand, still encased in the bulky glove. "Lieutenant Commander Jonathan Ford," the man said. "Executive officer, *seaQuest DSV*."

The other man had his helmet off too. "Weapons Officer Phillips," he said.

McShane shook their hands and took a breath. "We think that whoever planted the bombs is still down at the sub pool. They tried to get out, but we closed the gate."

Ford whispered. "And they didn't blow the place?"

"Guess they're considering other options."

Farrand, the SousMer director, stood next to McShane and spoke up. "There's an emergency opening, an override that will open the gate. Commander, they have one of our people with them. A hostage."

Ford nodded. "The way I see it, we're all hostages." He pulled on the strip that opened up his EVA suit and slipped his arms out. Phillips did the same.

"Are there any other explosives inside? Have you seen anything else?"

The director shrugged. "No, we haven't seen anything—and we've searched all over the ship."

Phillips nodded. "Can you give me some men? I can start sweeping the resort. I brought a low-density scanner that will pick up any bio-explosives, stuff you may have missed."

Ford spoke into a small microphone he disconnected from his helmet.

"Captain—we're on board, and proceeding with all speed."

Then Terry McShane heard Bridger's voice. "I can see that—better get going."

There was a pause.

"And give my regards to McShane."

Mary scrambled out, followed by Gooding.

"Come on, will you? Stop moving so bloody slowly."

This wasn't designed to be a suicide mission, and Mary had no intention of turning it into one.

Cutter popped his head up.

"Mary—I'm getting lots of traffic now. They're talking to *seaQuest* again. And there's something wrong with the SousMer computer system. I don't know. It's almost like—"

But Mary followed Gooding over to a pale blue console. Nothing was labeled, so she'd only have Gooding's word that these buttons could actually get the sea gate open.

"You know what to do here?"

Gooding nodded. "Sure. I only have to—"

"Hey—" Cutter's voice echoed eerily in the pool. "The whole system's down. Or something—"

"Open the gate now!" Mary said.

They ran, full out, to the back staircase.

Ford followed McShane, and behind them trailed three heavily armed SousMer guards who looked real nervous. They hadn't bargained for this . . .

"I hope you've used those guns before," Ford said to them. Everyone liked their rent-a-cops to carry the new electron-mag weapons. But not everyone made sure that they were trained to use them.

Ford opened a metal door and took the spiral staircase that bypassed the living quarters of the resort and twisted down to the sub pool.

And he thought:

In a few minutes this will be all over—or we'll all be dead.

Bridger stood up. "Come on, Lucas, tell me that you're—"

"I'm in, sir. Too cool—I'm *in*! It's our baby now. I'm inside the main programming unit of the resort. And now—wait a second—I do believe I'm even linked with the rogue computer inside. *Too much!*"

Bridger spoke to the air, while everyone on the bridge waited, breathlessly, listening to their own master hacker.

"Lucas . . . can you bring *that* computer down."

"Better, Captain. I can make it look like it's off-line for just a minute—there!—and then—everything's fine."

Bridger laughed. Gator was looking at him, a curious

expression on his face. "Everything's fine?"

"Yes, sir. Now the rogue computer is back on-line—except I'll see every command a few milliseconds before it's carried out."

Bridger walked over to Communications. "No word from Ford, Phillips?"

Bachmann shook his head. "Should I give them a buzz, Captain?"

"No. Let's just try to be patient . . ."

Bridger began pacing.

Phillips's scanner found the explosive within minutes. It wasn't hard, with the right scanning equipment, he knew. Too bad the resort didn't carry state-of-the-art stuff. They might not have been in this spot . . .

I bet the wine cellar can't be beat, he thought.

The director stood beside him and peered into the shaft. "Where does this go?" Phillips asked.

"Er, I'm not too sure—"

Another man came forward, obviously the engineer of the place. "That leads to the power plants."

"Is that bad?" Farrand said.

"It isn't good, sir," Phillips said, and he crawled into the shaft.

Ford stood next to McShane, outside two silvery doors.

"In here?" he whispered.

McShane nodded.

He held his breath. No telling what was waiting for them on the other side.

Ford turned to the SousMer guards. "On three . . . Ready . . . one . . . two—"

Cutter stood out of the sub's open hatch. "It's okay now. The computer's working fine. Don't know what happened—"

Mary turned to him and yelled. "Get back inside, Cutter. We're getting out of here as soon as the sea gate's open."

She saw Cutter nod. Then she saw him look up . . . and turn, as if he heard something, as if—

"What is it?" she said.

But then Mary heard the noise as doors to the sub pool flew open.

Harpe's assistant said, "The pilot wants direct confirmation, *voice* confirmation from you, Mr. Harpe."

And Geoffrey Harpe nodded. He walked over to the desk and took the headset from the woman.

"Hello, this is Geoffrey Harpe."

He heard the pilot's voice in his ear.

"Sir, I'd like you to confirm the order that I've been given."

"Yes, it's true. I want you to turn around immediately, return to—I don't know—I guess our Hong Kong airstrip would be the closest."

"But, sir, what about the drop, the gold?"

Harpe wasn't used to explaining things to employees.

"There will be no drop," Harpe said flatly. No need to explain that it would be throwing good money after bad, that the resort was probably doomed anyway. Best to look to the future . . .

The pilot didn't say anything.

"Could you acknowledge my order?" This was getting annoying.

"Yes, sir. I'm turning back now."

Harpe handed the headset back.

"What the—" Mary said, as she watched the people come into the pool area. "Get down!" she yelled at Cutter.

Standing there, so stupid, a liability now. A stupid target.

"The gate's open," Gooding said.

There was no way, Mary thought, no way to get to the sub, no way to get out—

"Freeze," a voice bellowed from the other end. "Don't move or touch anything. It's all over, just stay there."

Mary stood there. And yes, it did appear to be all over.

She looked at Gooding.

All over, unless . . .

She grabbed Gooding, yanked him close, and planted her gun flush against his head.

"No," she yelled back. "Don't try to stop us or I'll kill this man."

She started moving to the sub.

The people at the other end didn't move, only a moment's hesitation, a ripple of indecision—but enough for Mary to gain a few more steps to the sub.

She dragged Gooding one step, then another—closer to the sub entrance.

Ford stood there. "Who is that?" he said to McShane.

"He's with the resort."

"And he's not with them?"

"No—at least, they didn't think so."

One life, Ford thought, against all the lives inside the resort. Ford knew that Bridger was listening to every step, every movement.

"We've got to take them," Ford said quietly.

But McShane touched his arm. "See that man in the sub. He can probably set off the explosives. What about him?"

And, Ford thought, what about Phillips? Where was he?

"Captain," Ford said, speaking to Bridger. Timing was everything now. It all came down to time. "If you're ready, sir—I think we have to make our move."

The woman with the gun was only a few meters from the sub entrance . . . her stun gun held right against the side of the man's head.

Which was when something strange happened.

CHAPTER 10

They're going to get away, Gooding thought.

Yes, and then they'll blow us all up anyway—because they'll be away. All those people will die . . . and who's fault is that?

Who let that happen?

The gun pressed so hard against his head it hurt. He imagined what it would feel like to have the thin dart cut right into his head, with sleek, surgical precision.

It would be fast, Gooding thought.

Real fast, he hoped. And he decided that there was something that he had to do.

He pulled away from the woman, bucking his head, slipping out of her grasp.

Until he was—for a brief moment—free.

"Lucas, you still okay?" Bridger said.

"Everything looks great from here, Captain."

Then it must be time, Bridger knew. He looked over to Bachmann. "Tell Darwin—" Bridger took a breath. Then—

"Tell Darwin to *go!*"

Phillips crawled down the shaft. The low-density scanner picked up some kind of foreign material, possibly organic material down there. But—there was always the possibility that it wasn't an explosive, that there was only the charge placed outside.

Right, thought Phillips, but then what's in here? A dead rat?

Not too likely.

He kept shining the light in front of him, seeing nothing but the reflective glare of the metal shining back at him.

How much time do I have here? he thought. He imagined the tremendous blast, the tremendous force that would hit him if the explosive went off. Such a compact space would only magnify the explosive power.

A bad thought to have right now.

The Great Zucchini! Shot out of a service shaft in a never-done-before feat of—

He saw something. A little mudpie a few meters ahead, sitting on the bottom of the shaft. Pretty unobtrusive . . . But Phillips wasn't about to waste any time in appreciation of the terrorist's handiwork.

He moved his butt close to it as fast as he could do.

Darwin heard the two-word message . . .

Go . . . now!

With all the strength he could manage from his powerful back flipper, he shot in a straight line toward the object sitting on the side of the funny shaped building.

Darwin moved so fast, it seemed as if he might ram into it . . . until he pulled himself short and turned right in front of the bomb. He waited a moment, studying it. It didn't look like anything bad. It almost looked like one of those sea stars from the island, before the *seaQuest,* before there were *words* . . .

Then Darwin reached out and grabbed the explosive in his beak—

And sped away.

"God—no!" Cutter yelled from the sub's hatch.

Mary twisted and tried to grab Gooding, but the man slipped away, backed away against the wall.

Then she did what she had promised.

She fired her gun at him, and Gooding collapsed to the ground. Then she turned and saw the others coming toward her. Mary took aim and fired.

There was no smoke, no blast, just a pencil-thin line of tracer light heading toward the target, as the electron dart fired and one of the guards fell to the ground.

Cutter—stupid man!—kept yelling at her. "Someone touched the explosive outside," he yelled. "It's going to blow!"

What would stupid Cutter do if they captured him? What could he tell them about Rafael?

So Mary's next shot was aimed at Cutter's head. His face was filled with a pathetic horror as the electron dart hit.

Then she quickly fell to the ground and crawled behind the console. Above her head she heard the crystalline sound of darts—return fire—hitting the steel walls.

It doesn't matter, she thought. *We're all dead . . . in only seconds.*

Lucas sat at the keyboard. He saw the message being transmitted that the explosive had been touched, a message heading to whatever portable VR unit the terrorists had been using. The message would take only a few milliseconds, and then there would be the detonation, automatic once the message was received.

Lucas took the message and fed it into a loop.

"Here we go," he said. "Sending it up to the Net." He had built a path for the message made up of *millions* of electronic pathways, as the message searched for access to its home computer, for acknowledgment.

With luck, it might buy eight seconds.

And God—thought Lucas—if only that was enough time.

Phillips looked at the flat patty, the explosive.

He saw the microchip, the detonator, sitting in the middle of the bluish pie. And just as he was about to pry the detonator loose, he heard something, a *hum*—as if it were armed, ready, waiting.

"What the—" he said, his voice echoing in the narrow chamber.

Something was happening.

He took two tiny tweezers and brought them close to the chip. Couldn't rush this, had to pull it out smoothly, like a surgeon.

One tweezer closed on one end of the chip. Then he placed the other tweezer on the other side, grabbing the chip very gently. If the detonator were programmed to be movement sensitive, it would all be over in seconds.

But—Phillips tried to reassure himself—they wouldn't do that. They wouldn't think anyone would find this. And there'd be too much jostling around getting the damn explosive in here.

He tried to convince himself.

Okay, lift off . . . , he thought, gently disengaging the tiny detonator from the explosive.

Until it *popped* free, the organic explosive making a sucking noise.

And yes—the detonator was definitely making the tiniest little humming sound.

Darwin counted.

Four seconds . . . five seconds . . . He looked back, but he still could see the strange underwater building, the thing he was saving . . . and it still seemed to him that he was too close to let the bomb go.

So he kicked even harder, faster to get away.

Harder, faster—

"Talk to me, Lucas, tell me what's happening."

Lucas heard Bridger's voice. But Lucas was watching the clock, watching his computer track the paths as the acknowledgment code traveled around the world's communication networks, once, twice—

Five seconds . . . six seconds . . .

Darwin should have dropped the explosive, should be

getting out of the area by now, Lucas thought.

"Come on, Dar. Drop it . . . ," Lucas hissed.

"What's that?" Bridger said.

But—at least for the next two seconds—Lucas couldn't talk. He could only watch the clock.

The chip was free. Great, thought Phillips, but what if it has a mini-explosive built into it, for moments just like this?

Phillips gulped. It was always a possibility.

He crawled backward, away from the explosive, and, when he couldn't see the pie-shaped object anymore, he took the chip and smashed it against the side wall of the shaft.

He was relieved to hear that the minute humming sound had stopped.

Six seconds . . . seven seconds . . .

Maybe *now,* thought Darwin, looking back, and seeing that the resort was sheltered by a rocky ridge, and that the building was blurry, the funny building nearly lost in the darkness.

Darwin dropped the explosive, letting it begin its fall to the even deeper abyss below.

Eight . . .

And *there,* Lucas saw that Darwin had at last released the explosive—exactly when it was supposed to explode.

But then it was nine seconds . . .

Still okay. Still no boom.

"Come on, Darwin. Swim like you've never swam before . . ."

Ten seconds . . .

"Lucas," the Captain said.

But then the shock wave of the blast hit *seaQuest.*

Darwin reached the rocky ridge and quickly swooped down when the explosion went off. And the dolphin felt the water, a strange current rushing over him, sending him spinning, swirling out of control.

Darwin screeched. The water had a bad taste to it, and it was warm.

The current smashed Darwin into some rock, still twisting, turning—

Then into more rocks, and the dolphin felt his skin tear against the jagged edges.

The sub pool rocked under the blast, but—after a moment—Ford realized that they were still here, still intact, still in one piece.

Not a bad feeling, he thought.

When he looked up he saw the woman—Mary Knox—making her way to the sub. The water in the pool rippled, showing small spit curls after the blast.

The woman was only feet from the submersible. She was nothing if not determined.

Ford stood up to get a better shot at her.

But then she shot at Ford, and he felt the heat from her tracer light touch his cheek. She was no amateur with her gun, he knew.

She clambered on top of the small sub, almost at the hatch.

Ford maybe had time for one more shot.

He aimed at her head, the only spot not protected by the kelvar armor she wore. She turned and looked at him. And Ford saw awareness in her eyes.

Ford *fired.* And as if she were merely sleeping, the woman slumped over, half in, half out of the sub.

Ford stood there a moment, and then he said, "It's over . . . It's all over down here, Captain."

"Captain," Bachmann said, "I'm not getting anything from Darwin."

"Lucas—what about it . . . what can you tell me?"

For a moment, Lucas didn't respond. Bridger waited. The entire crew on the bridge stood there, listening . . .

"He's not responding—I'm not getting anything, Captain. He should have dropped the explosives at six seconds, seven the max. He got to eight before he dropped it and it exploded at ten. He was lucky, Captain, but he was awfully close . . ."

Bridger listened, thinking, *Is this the world I've been pulled back into? A world where you lose what you love?*

I've been here before, Bridger thought. *And I thought I'd left it forever.*

The cavalry to the rescue and, hey, we only lose a dolphin. Not so bad, eh? That's not such a bad deal . . .

"Captain," Crocker said. "Do you want to send a team out to look for Darwin?"

"Why—to pick up the pieces?" Bridger snapped. Right now, he hated everything and everyone connected to *seaQuest.* "I don't—"

"Wait a second. I'm getting something, some movement—Captain," Ortiz said, "Junior has a visual, outside the ship."

It couldn't be . . .

"Let's see it," Bridger said.

One of the screens flickered, turned to snow as it linked up with the video feed from Junior, and then—

There was Darwin.

"Nathan, he looks wounded."

"I see, Gator. Pull him in through one of the forward dive chambers. Looks like he's cut up—get the doctor to take a look."

"And Darwin lost his communication harness," Bachmann said.

Yes, thought Bridger, *and now he looks like an ordinary dolphin, hurt but—please God—alive.* Bridger smiled.

"Er, Captain, UEO calling, they're wondering—"

"They can wait, Lieutenant." And Bridger went forward to see how his old friend was doing.

Dr. Richard Ernst recognized that he was more than a bit drunk.

It was over. He could see people laughing, the SousMer staff smiling, reassuring people. It was all *over. We're not going to die,* he thought.

And Ernst began to think of what he had to do, now that he had his life back again.

He had to get to a VR link. Check on the status of the project. See how he was going to get the hell out of there.

And coffee, thought Ernst. *I need lots and lots of coffee.*

He pulled himself to his feet and rejoined the land of the living, knowing that the real difficult times, the real problems, were still ahead.

TWO

A Fire in the Sea

CHAPTER 11

Bridger called the meeting for one hour after the resort was declared "secure."

There were no more explosives and no more terrorists, but there were loose ends to be tied up, storm reports coming in, and updates on Darwin's condition.

"I don't care where I am," he had told Shimura. "I want to know what's up with Darwin. Interrupt me and keep me posted about his condition."

Though Dr. Akira Shimura was the ship's doctor, the ship's *human* doctor, he was also experienced working with cetaceans.

"I even saved an Orca baby once, when the mother had been accidentally killed," Shimura said. "It was the most amazing thing . . . The mother had been rammed by a research ship . . . and I was able to deliver her baby. Incredible experience."

Shimura always touched his arm when he talked, Bridger knew, as if the doctor were constantly aware that the artificial skin that he had generated there wasn't really part of him.

Shimura brought a lot of compassion to his work with Darwin.

"It looks good," he told Bridger. "The wound isn't so bad."

Now Bridger sat in the SousMer director's conference room, around a rosewood table shaped like a breaking wave. It was important to get all the loose details locked up and send the UEO a nice, neat report.

He had even navigated the first hello to Terry McShane pretty well, he thought.

"Thanks, Terry," he had said. "Having you inside helped." He was also curious what she was doing inside . . . but that could wait for later.

Now, he found himself avoiding her eyes, perhaps avoiding some old feelings that hadn't died.

"I want to commend you for everything." Bridger started talking to the SousMer people and the *seaQuest* crew. "A major disaster was averted by your very brave action." He looked at Phillips and, especially, Ford—whose eyes still looked bright with the excitement of the shoot-out at the moon pool. "Commander Ford and Lieutenant Phillips . . . Ms. McShane of the UEO, your security crew, Monsieur Farrand . . ." Bridger took a breath.

"I think it's safe to say that we're all here, safe and sound, because everyone kept their cool. Now, I have a few questions, some details to go over for my report. Our words will be recorded for audio only, if you don't mind. And I'm afraid this may take a while, so if anyone wants to grab some coffee, or—"

He saw Ford grin. *Bet he wishes he had a cold beer, like me,* Bridger thought. *Perhaps we'll crack some of the Captain's private stock when we get back . . .*

"Okay, let's start with the initial security check. I suppose—"

Jacques Farrand looked discomfited. He raised his hand, and Bridger had to smile at the gesture. This wasn't third grade . . .

"Monsieur le Directeur?"

"Captain—I am sorry. But my staff tells me that the people, our guests . . . many of them want to leave SousMer immediately."

Bridger rubbed his chin. *When's the next ferry due?*

That was the trouble with an underwater resort . . . You couldn't simply hop a plane and fly back to the mainland.

"So—you are arranging passage?"

Farrand grimaced. "That is just it, Captain. This storm, this 'Mike.' "

Phillips laughed. Bridger shot him a glance. There was a lot of nervous energy to be blown off. Still, he didn't want his officers laughing at the poor man.

"The tropical storm?"

"Yes, it has closed all the facilities on the island. No one will get to leave for a couple of days, perhaps more—"

Bridger nodded. "So tell your guests. I'm sure"—now Bridger grinned at his exec—"Mr. Harpe will 'comp' them after being through a stressful experience."

Farrand nodded.

Bridger felt Terry watching him. *Am I showing off for her?* he wondered. *Here I am, all of thirteen again. Look at me, I'm Captain of the biggest, baddest submarine in the world. I just saved six hundred people, and—God—*

He thought, *She still looks beautiful.*

It bothered him then. Why was she here? It was doubtful that this was her idea of a vacation. And it seemed a bit convenient that a UEO security chief was at SousMer when the guano hit the fan.

"A few guests," Farrand went on timidly, "have suggested, that since you are here, that the *seaQuest* is *here*, it could transport them to Flamingo."

Flamingo on the Florida Gulf coast. The commercial sub base there catered to both undersea mining and the day-trippers out for a look at the abyss.

Bridger shook his head. "Sorry, Monsieur Farrand, the *seaQuest* may be many things—but it's not a commercial transport. I'm afraid your guests—"

"They are some very important people, Monsieur Captain."

I bet, thought Bridger. And some of them probably didn't

97

want the world's eyes on them when they emerged with their mistresses and rent-a-hunks. He could see Senator Eleanor Bell, who, it was rumored, was on the guest list, emerging with a young stud in tow.

"Oh, he's only my personal trainer . . ."

And I'm Captain Nemo.

"I'm afraid it's out of the question, Monsieur Farrand. Now, Mr. Phillips, you have checked the facility for any other explosive material, of any kind?"

Phillips was whispering to Ford. He sat up straight to answer his captain's question.

"Er, yes, sir." And Bridger sat back to listen to Phillips's report.

"Mr. Harpe—"

Geoffrey Harpe looked out to the deserted pool, where no sign of his wonderful party remained. The Hawaiian sky was perfectly clear. A nearly full moon spread a milky white on perfectly cut glass, painting the palms gray.

"Mr. Harpe," his communications person said again.

It had been quite a day, and—he guessed—the ending wasn't too bad. The bullion was safe and sound. The resort saved. There was only one downside.

"I've got more messages for you, sir, from the UEO, and three more—all marked urgent—from MacInnis."

Harpe nodded. The downside was that it was the *seaQuest* that had to rescue everyone, that Nathan Hale Bridger—once again—was the good guy.

What was the alternative? he thought. For everyone to die and take the bloody *seaQuest* with them?

I couldn't want that. I couldn't be that sick.

He turned to the communications tech. Maria . . . Marla . . . something like that. A native islander, and she was pretty, sitting in the light of the three VR monitors, a festive Christmas display of lights.

Very pretty, but Harpe made it a rule never to push *that* button with his employees. He wondered how long she had been working. Someone else would come soon to relieve her, to stand watch over his empire . . . someone else whose name he wasn't quite sure of . . .

"Do you want to view the messages, sir?"

Harpe nodded.

"Do you wish them to be private communications, sir?"

Again Harpe nodded, and he walked over to the console and picked up a pair of lightweight, wireless VR lenses and put them on.

"Okay. I'm ready. Put the UEO message on first."

Inside the lenses, the Harpe WorldWide Enterprises logo gave way to a three-dimensional image of Admiral Noyce.

"Mr. Harpe, what exactly were you doing out there, with that transport? You never told us that you turned the damned plane around. What if we hadn't been able—"

No need to hear any more of this, Harpe thought. "Next one," he said.

This only took a few seconds, and then Harpe saw Ralph MacInnis talking to him from a site about two hundred miles west of the Azores . . . and over thirty-four hundred feet below the surface.

MacInnis, Chief of Research, stood in his office.

He was a good scientist, but even better at looking at the bottom line.

"Mr. Harpe, I'm afraid I have bad news to report—"

The image flipped, and Harpe was looking at a hydrothermal vent field—rows of chimneys, black smokers gushing poisonous hydrogen sulfides, and stretching past them, fields of the giant tube worms, tree-trunk-thick bodies tinged with pink—

The pinkish color came from hemoglobin, Harpe knew.

That fact still blew Harpe's mind.

The view was from one of the research base's submersibles.

"We lost a sub in the area on your screen, Mr. Harpe. We're still checking into what happened. But there doesn't appear—"

MacInnis's face was back, looking nervous.

Easy, boy, Harpe thought. *Not every day you discover something brand new, a brand new life-form, something so ancient that it could—*

MacInnis rubbed his chin. Harpe wondered if perhaps

this deep-sea pro were not the right man for the job. And MacInnis better remember not to say anything, not through normal Net communications—

MacInnis looked away worried. "Everything else . . . appears okay, Mr. Harpe. We're looking into what happened to the sub." The message was over.

"Reply?" the communications person asked.

"You say there's more?"

"Two more—they all came in while you were dealing with the SousMer situation, sir. We held them, as you requested."

"No reply to this. But let me see what else came in."

There was another blip inside the goggles, and then MacInnis was there again—

Looking scared.

"God, Mr. Harpe. This is incredible. This is—"

Then there was a shot from the base's main sub pool, tight on the twisted wreckage of a submersible.

Harpe felt his heart start beating. And yes, he had to admit that what he heard, what MacInnis proceeded to say, was truly . . . *incredible.*

Rafael Vargas looked at the live news feed from EarthNet.

"The UEO has not yet released the name of the terrorists who threatened the SousMer Underwater Resort of Geoffrey Harpe."

Ozawa, Rafael's first mate—formerly of the Japanese navy—stood close by.

"But it has been confirmed that the two terrorists inside the resort, a man and a woman, are dead. UEO director Admiral William Noyce has announced a worldwide search for the terrorists' accomplices, a group believed to be headed by Rafael Var—"

"Off," Rafael said.

The news feed vanished.

"Plot a course, Ozawa. Get us the hell out of this damned trench before they find that we're hiding here."

Ozawa nodded. "Yes, sir. Where are—?"

"Anywhere, Mr. Ozawa. Anywhere we won't be found . . ."

Ozawa started giving navigation orders to the crew of the modified Skipjack, a submarine loaded with plasma torpedoes.

Rafael promised himself: There would come a reckoning on this matter.

He couldn't imagine Mary dead. The iron woman.

How could anyone kill her? She was too strong . . .

Yes, there would come a reckoning . . . with the *seaQuest* . . . and with her captain, Nathan Bridger.

But—for now—that could wait.

"So," Bridger said, "that about wraps it up. We've got all the information from your computer, Monsieur Director."

Farrand looked surprised.

"We linked up before my men even came on board."

Bridger looked at McShane. There were questions he wanted to ask her, questions about what had happened here, why she was here—

Something else is going on here.

And other questions, about her life since they last met.

But those questions could wait.

"If there's nothing else, Captain, I'd like to attend to my guests."

Ford looked over and caught Bridger's eye. The lieutenant stood up. "Captain, I guess—if there's nothing else—we'd better get back to the ship."

Bridger nodded. Phillips stood up and, with Bridger's exec, headed for the door. "Oh—Mr. Ford . . . Lieutenant Phillips . . ."

The two men paused.

"Gentlemen—you did *good*."

"Thank you, sir," Ford said.

"Oh—and plot that course to the Canal. Might as well get back on our planned itinerary. San Francisco here we come . . ."

"Aye, aye, sir."

The two men left, and—Bridger was left alone with the only woman he ever had an affair with . . .

Harpe had replayed the three messages from MacInnis before he spoke to the UEO. Noyce had left the office complex, Harpe was told, but the Admiral was reached in his car via a handheld unit.

And Harpe outlined the problem to him.

He told the Admiral what had happened in the Azores vent area. And what the problem was at the Azores Deep-Sea Research Base.

Harpe spoke quietly, softly . . .

"Admiral, this could go way beyond bomb threats . . . and six hundred lives—*way* beyond."

He saw Noyce's face turn grim while Harpe told him all the information that—until this moment—had been such a carefully guarded secret.

And where Harpe didn't know the answers to Noyce's questions, he made them up. Because, well, the important thing was to get the wheels in motion.

When Harpe was done, Noyce didn't need any more convincing.

Terry McShane stood up. "There are things I'd better attend to, Nate."

But he walked over to her and grabbed her arm, grinning.

"Now—wait a second. You don't walk away from this room without giving me some answers."

When his hand touched her arm, it was a strange, electric moment. In a flash, the years passed away—and he remembered the last time he had touched her.

Bridger always thought of it as an affair, and he had felt the requisite amount of guilt over it.

He and Barbara had been working apart. Their son was a young teenager—and growing more difficult by the day. Communication wasn't good. It happened, Bridger supposed, in every relationship . . .

But then he met Terry McShane. She had graduated to Naval Intelligence from the CIA's Internal Affairs Division. She didn't talk much about her job, but when they were alone, Bridger referred to her as a "spy" and she didn't exactly deny it.

They both shared a vision of the ocean as a new frontier, a new world that could be used for the benefit of the planet—or exploited by those who wanted to make a buck.

They were both passionate about the subject, and Bridger, working in Norfolk and commuting home to Washington on weekends, didn't see the telltale signs that something else was happening between them.

There were dinners, and drinks, and sharing life stories—and Bridger never saw the danger signs in Terry's blue-green eyes.

They only made love once.

Though he had relived that night many times since.

They had made love, and Bridger knew that they couldn't ever do that again. Not if he wanted to keep his life, his family. He didn't know that something else was going to take that all away from him.

He and Terry agreed to "stay friends." But he knew it was only his agreement, that Terry McShane had felt betrayed.

Somehow, she got transferred from Norfolk to the West Coast . . . and he never saw her again.

Though he had thought of her many times since then.

Now, here she was, and he was touching her arm.

She looked down at his hand.

"What do you want to know, Captain?"

"Oh, come on . . . Don't give me that 'Captain' stuff. And don't tell me that you were down here for a little vacation. This Disney waterworld for grown-ups with big bucks isn't your style."

"You know . . . I'm working for the UEO—same as you," she smiled. "That should be enough."

She hasn't forgotten or forgiven me, Nathan saw.

It was so *cold* in there it stung.

"Sure, we're coworkers . . . and that's why I'm asking what you're doing here."

"I don't think I can tell you."

Bridger studied her. But he knew that as much as he pushed, she wouldn't budge. "Okay . . . I understand. Security and all that." He shook his head and turned away. "I'll call up Bill Noyce and get him to tell me."

"I don't think—"

"Captain Bridger—"

Someone's voice—from SousMer Communications—was on the loudspeaker.

"Right here," he said.

"We have a request from a Chief Crocker for you to return to the bridge of the *seaQuest*. He says it's important."

"News about Darwin?" Terry asked.

"Could be . . . I'll let you know." Bridger turned and quickly left the conference room.

CHAPTER 12

Sitting in the *seaQuest*'s transport sub, Bridger was tempted to call the bridge and ask what was so damn important that he had to hurry back. But there had to be a good reason that Crocker—in charge while he and Ford were off the ship—hadn't told him that reason.

Perhaps security was involved, and now Bridger's imagination kicked in. Maybe there was a renegade sub in the area, he thought. Perhaps the elusive Rafael himself wanted to attack the resort, or *seaQuest*.

But that wasn't too likely. Rafael hadn't stayed free by being stupid. His plan was a good one—only he hadn't banked on the *seaQuest* getting involved, and he certainly hadn't planned on his two people in the resort getting trapped.

Did Rafael have a second target?

That would make sense. Two targets would make it certain that he'd catch the UEO by complete surprise.

Bridger sat in the transport for the five-minute shuttle from the resort to the moon pool of the *seaQuest*.

Then a third possibility occurred to him.

It's Darwin. Darwin didn't make it, and Gator wants to tell me to my face.

Sure—that could be it.

Bridger nodded. *Because I'm supposed to lose everything I care about.*

The sleek black shape of *seaQuest* was visible ahead, the hull of the sub almost lost in the abyssal darkness. He saw the glow from the bridge and the running lights that gilded the exterior, outlining the blackish-blue of the cyclic polymer surface.

The ship looked more like a living thing, a giant phosphorescent hammerhead.

And like a living thing, Bridger thought, *it has bitten out of my life.*

Lieutenant Commander Ford was already on duty by the time Bridger got up to the bridge. He was talking to Crocker, who rubbed his chin the way he always did whenever he dealt with something disagreeable.

"Where's the fire?" Bridger said.

Crocker didn't smile. It was the same face the SOB had worn when they used to play poker years ago. No grins until the last card was triumphantly played.

"What, no smiles?"

The waiting was almost over . . .

"Captain," Ford started.

"Sir," Crocker jumped in, "we got a security code one message from the UEO. For your eyes only."

It wasn't about Darwin—and Bridger breathed a bit easier.

There was nothing that Bridger would keep secret from Crocker about this ship. As his chief of the helm, Bridger trusted him completely. And the same went for Ford.

Still, he'd better see what the message was privately.

"I'll check it in my cabin. I could use a hot shower and change of clothes . . ."

Hurrying, Bridger went to his stateroom, his curiosity prodding him along.

▲   ▲   ▲

A face on the VR screen in his cabin asked for his identification.

"Captain Nathan Hale Bridger." Bridger paused, and then gave his UEO Security number. "8-0-1-7-3-1."

The screen flashed, "Voice Recognition and Security Code Confirmed."

And then Bill Noyce was on the screen, looking as if it were a live feed.

And why wasn't it a live feed? Bridger wondered. Why didn't Noyce contact him directly and speak with him? Curiouser and curiouser . . .

"Captain," Noyce said.

A bit formal, Bridger thought. What's going on here? *Didn't I just save the UEO's—*

"There's been a change in the orders for the *seaQuest*."

Good, thought Bridger, *I didn't want to go to San Francisco anyway, parade past the Golden Gate Bridge and let VIPs poke around the ship. Certainly there was something more useful we could be doing.*

"There's a scientist at SousMer who will require transport to the UEO Deep-Sea Research Station in the Azores."

"Transport?" Bridger said aloud to the screen. "Give me a break. Now we're a bus?"

The message continued . . .

"The scientist's name is Dr. Richard Ernst of Der Berliner Akademie für Wissenschaft. He is to be transported, with all due speed, to the research station. Further, Captain, you are to remain at the station while Dr. Ernst conducts his inspection of the facility."

Then Bridger saw something odd. Noyce hesitated—as if he were about to say something else, something that would clue Bridger in to what the hell was really going on here . . .

"Er, Nathan, you are to lend Dr. Ernst whatever support necessary while doing what you must to guarantee the security of the *seaQuest*."

Guarantee the security of the seaQuest*?*

Bridger had about a dozen questions, but at the top of the list was, Why couldn't this Dr. Ernst use a normal sub transport, some commercial vehicle on a milk run out of Florida or Rio? Wasn't using the *seaQuest* a bit of overkill?

Of course, he couldn't ask questions of a recorded message.

"Nathan—"

Noyce was softening, letting his authoritative mask slip a bit. *Probably,* Bridger thought, *because he can imagine the steam coming from my ears.*

"You will be traveling to the largest hydrothermal vent area ever discovered, a relatively new area that has been off-limits to all commercial interests. Not only is the field extensive, the topography of the area is dangerous, with the thirty acres of vent site dotted with dangerous volcanic deposits and subterranean caves. Dr. Ernst will be able to brief your team fully once he's aboard and you're under way."

Noyce took a breath. "Be careful, Nathan."

Bridger was about to address the screen and command it to go off—the message was surely finished—when Noyce added something.

"Oh—I have also ordered Terry McShane to come on board the ship. She will observe the interaction of the naval and scientific units on *seaQuest* and prepare a report for the UEO. It's something the board would like to see. Have a safe voyage, Nathan."

Noyce disappeared, and the words "Message Completed" flashed.

"What the—" Bridger took out his VR-PAL, the easiest way to communicate while walking to the bridge. "Bachmann, get me someone, *anyone,* at the UEO."

"Aye, aye, Captain. Sir, we've also had a request from SousMer to ferry over two civilians . . . for transport, sir. Should I begin processing that request?"

"No," Bridger barked.

He ran to the bridge, past the empty tank where Darwin often followed him like a frisky puppy. *God, I still haven't checked on Darwin . . .*

All eyes fell on Bridger when he got to the bridge. "Orders, sir?" Ford said.

"In a minute, Mr. Ford. Bachmann, are we through to the UEO yet?"

"No, sir . . . The Net is running slow. The weather playing havoc with signal use."

"Keep at it."

Crocker stood to the side. "Anything you care to pass along, Captain?"

"Maybe, Gator. I only have to check on a few things."

"Sir," Bachmann said, "another request. The two parties at SousMer—Dr. Ernst and Ms. McShane—report that they have UEO clearance to come on board."

Bridger smiled. *Whose ship was this anyway?* he thought. "In a minute, Lieutenant."

"Sir—I have a link to UEO Command now. Center screen."

There was a face that Bridger had never seen before, a young man with short blond hair and cold blue eyes.

"Could you put me through to Admiral Noyce, please?"

"Sir—I'm afraid I can't—"

"Look—" Bridger saw the man's name—Captain Gerry Wilson, communications officer. "Look, Gerry, wherever the Admiral is, he can be reached, and I'm sure he'll want to speak—"

But Gerry shook his head. "Captain, he left explicit instructions not to be disturbed for the next sixteen hours. As you can imagine, he's quite exhausted by the crisis at—"

"Well, I'm not exactly feeling well rested myself, Gerry. If this Dr. Ernst needs transport somewhere, then surely you can arrange—"

"Captain Bridger, Tropical Storm Mike is a major storm system. You can check EarthNet to see the tremendous damage it's doing. There are literally no surface ports open; nothing is moving anywhere. And any subs we have at sea are rushing to aid devastated areas. The *seaQuest* is the closest vessel to the area."

"And Dr. Ernst can't wait?"

Gerry's face was rigid, implacable. He took a breath. *What's going on here?* Bridger thought.

"No, sir. He can't."

For a moment, Bridger was tempted to tell Communications Officer Gerry Wilson that he had no intention of following that order, that if they wanted the *seaQuest* to be a bus, then they could get another captain.

But there was something very odd about this. Noyce unavailable, McShane coming aboard, and—above it all—the feeling that something strange was going on at the UEO Deep-Sea Research Base in the Azores.

Noyce's recorded words came back to him . . .

. . . while doing what you must to guarantee the security of the seaQuest.

Secure from what?

Bridger was curious—and he had never believed the old saw that curiosity killed the cat.

He turned to Lieutenant Bachmann.

"Permission to board . . . granted, Mr. Bachmann."

Dr. Akira Shimura's medical center looked more like a greenhouse. Besides the dozens of exotic plants he had growing—from genetically-altered bromeliads to rare orchids, *in full bloom*—Shimura also had tanks holding assorted underwater algae, including containers of phytoplankton and spirogyra. Shimura owed these simple-celled plants and animals his continued existence.

Bridger saw the doctor leaning into a large holding tank. Some of Shimura's cancer-ravaged organs had been exchanged for transplants that depended on tissue created from the plankton and plant material.

It worked well enough, except for one limitation. Shimura could never leave the protective, controlled atmosphere of *seaQuest* or, as he told Bridger, the skinlike material would quickly begin to decay.

"I'm alive, but a prisoner for life."

Bridger suspected that the man wasn't that unhappy with his plight. His plants, his work, were his life. And, as Shimura often said, "Who could not be happy with all the Earth's oceans to explore?"

Shimura didn't hear Bridger enter.

"Akira . . ."

Shimura looked quickly, then turned back to the tank. "Yes, Nathan. Come closer, I think you should see . . . this."

Bridger pushed past a trio of grasping spider plants dangling from the overhead lights. Chances were this medical room was in violation of any number of UEO codes.

As if anyone would report Shimura.

Bridger came closer and saw Darwin on his side, with his breathing hole and one filmy eye out of the water. The eye seemed to widen when it saw Bridger, and the Captain instinctively looked up to the speaker, expecting Darwin to greet him.

"Oh," Shimura said. "I had to remove the communications linkup, the microtransmitter. Not for long, but it was positioned in a delicate spot."

Darwin stirred in the tank.

"Easy, boy, easy," Shimura said. "He might get very excited when he sees you. I have given him medication, painkiller, a light sedative. He was sleeping a little while ago."

"Can he hear us, understand us?"

"Oh, yes."

Bridger came close to the tank. He scooped up a handful of water and dribbled it along the side of Darwin's head. Then he smoothed the skin. Darwin's eye blinked, and then the dolphin stirred in the tank.

"Easy, Dar," Bridger said. And then the Captain saw the wound, an open patch of whitish fat and tissue just behind the great head of the dolphin.

Bridger winced, and he caught Shimura looking at him. "I know, it looks bad. I was worried . . . I thought there could be damage to his nervous system; you see the wound is so close to the dolphin's backbone. They are so much like us, it is such a vital area."

"Then, he's okay?"

Shimura nodded. "I have cleaned the wound. There were bits of, I don't know, debris from the explosion, bits of rock. I also treated the wound with a solvent made up

111

of zooplankton tissue cells. They will protect the opening while it heals. In a day or so, I'll put a water-resistant bandage on the wound—just to keep it protected. Then I can put back the communicator chip, and Darwin should be nearly as good as new."

Again the dolphin kicked up the water, splashing its big tail out and wetting Bridger and Shimura.

They laughed, and Bridger said, "Yes, that is good news, eh, boy?"

Shimura grinned. "Now, you'd best leave, Captain, and let the patient get some rest."

Lieutenant Commander Ford escorted the two "guests" to the bridge. Ford saw that they both looked around the bridge, in awe of the electronic wonderland that was the heart of the *seaQuest*.

"Why is everything lit with a turquoise light?" Terry McShane asked. Ford knew nothing about her, except that she was with the UEO and she was coming on board. That was enough to have him on his toes.

"The ambient light reflects the situation of the ship, Ms. McShane. The blue indicates the lowest level of alert, normal cruising conditions. In the case of a conflict or other emergency, the interior lighting would reflect the condition."

"So—it serves a psychological purpose?" the scientist, Dr. Ernst, asked. Ernst didn't look so good, Ford thought. Whatever he had done to weather the hostage incident had left him looking bedraggled.

"Psychological and informational. The color change can affect how the crew responds to situations; it provides information as to the level of alertness. Different procedures are followed at different levels, from blue to green, to yellow—"

"But there is also a psychological component?"

"Yes, I imagine there is."

Ford looked down the port passageway and saw Captain Bridger hurrying to them. *Just in time,* Ford thought. He didn't like having these two civilians on the bridge, what used to be *his* bridge, asking all these questions.

Let the Captain deal with them.

And was it only his imagination, Ford thought, or did he sense a tenseness coming from McShane?

Was there some history here? Between her and Bridger?

Well, wouldn't that make the next few days even more interesting . . .

CHAPTER 3

CHAPTER 13

Bridger walked up to the scientist. "Dr. Ernst, Captain Bridger."

"Captain—" Ernst said.

Bridger looked over at Terry McShane and nodded. "And nice to see you again, Ms. McShane."

She smiled at his formality, and it was good to see her grin.

Bridger turned to his exec. "We'd better get going. Mr. Ford—if you've set a course, trim forward ballast . . ."

Ford relayed the order.

"Ahead one-half. Set aft dive planes—"

"Captain," Ernst interrupted, "I was told that you could provide me with a console and a communications unit. There are—"

"Yes, Dr. Ernst—but there's one thing you should understand." Bridger glanced at Ford, who took a breath as if bracing himself for the storm to follow. Bridger's warm smile gave no clue to his words to come . . .

"What I'd like you to understand, Dr. Ernst, is that I don't want you here and I don't want to ferry you to the vent area."

"But you have been ordered—"

Bridger raised a hand. "Yes, yes, I know. I've been *ordered* to take you to the Azores Research Base. And so— I will. But I don't have to pretend to be happy about it."

"I must have a console to link up with the base."

Bridger nodded to Ford. "Lieutenant Bachmann, my communications officer, will see that you get everything you need. And—" Bridger looked at Terry. "And we'll prepare quarters for you and Ms. McShane. But, if you don't mind my suggesting, we have over a day's sailing before we reach the base. We've all been through a lot, and rest—for all of us—might be in order."

Bridger took a breath.

"Perhaps, Dr. Ernst, you could prepare a briefing for me on the vent area we're going to. Say, eleven o'clock—that's in the morning."

"I know what time—"

"As for me, if I don't get some sleep, my head's going to explode. Mr. Ford, see that our course is plotted and logged. And the helm is yours—"

Bridger turned around and walked away . . . "And don't wake me."

There were no dreams this time, no bittersweet fantasies that were so real he could almost touch them.

Bridger slept soundly, awakening only when he heard a noise in the passageway. He blinked himself alert in the dark stateroom.

He flapped around with his hand, searching for a light switch. "Lights," he said, still not quite used to the fact that so much on this ship was voice-responsive. The room was instantly lit. He looked at the clock on the sleek Lucite desk that projected out of the wall. 8:45.

Not enough sleep, Bridger thought. He certainly didn't feel rested.

But it was time he got up. He actually looked forward to hearing Ernst's presentation on the vent area . . . and, even more than that, he looked forward to seeing Terry McShane again.

He showered, shaved, and, while he did, he studied his face in the mirror, the added lines and cracks. No longer young, not quite old.

Too old to be feeling this odd rush of adrenaline thinking about Terry, he thought.

Before he headed down to the officers' mess, he stopped at the bridge and checked that everything was fine, the *seaQuest* moving at a steady 110 knots toward the Azores, with nothing eventful having happened during the night.

Then Bridger went down to breakfast.

Terry McShane sat alone. It looked as if she had just finished eating and was ready to leave.

Bridger walked over to her.

"Hope you're not leaving."

She looked up, no smile on her face. "Leaving the ship? I don't think that's a possibility."

Bridger sat down at the table. "You don't seem too friendly this morning."

One of the cooks came over holding a pot of coffee and a cup on a saucer.

"Coffee, Captain?"

"Yes, thank you," Bridger said.

He watched Terry while the cook poured the coffee. They waited—and when the man was gone, they both started speaking at the same time. And now finally—she smiled.

"No," Bridger said. "You go first. I insist."

The smile stayed there, a sweet smile that fit her auburn hair, her sparkling green eyes.

"It's obvious you don't want me here, Nathan."

"Oh, I wouldn't go that far. Let's say that I don't know *why* you're here. And I don't like being told who can come on my ship."

"Your ship?"

Now it was Bridger's turn to grow serious. "What this ship is, and what it can become . . . a force to make the oceans a place to live and work, a ship that will discover secrets we can only dream of." He took a sip of the coffee. "That's my ship."

117

"The UEO might disagree on ownership."

Bridger smiled again. "They probably would. Now, why don't you tell me—what are you really doing here?"

Lieutenant Hitchcock and Lieutenant Krieg came into the mess, talking loudly. But, looking over at their captain, they quieted down.

Terry looked at Bridger. "You know why I'm on—"

"Okay," he smiled. "Sure . . . to study the interaction of the military and scientific crews. So don't tell me the real reason. When you're good and ready, I'll be here."

There was silence again, and there was this feeling, this terrible desire to say things that, maybe, should have been said a long time ago.

Their eyes locked, and—for one powerful moment—the beauty and feeling in Terry's eyes was enough to make Bridger want to reach out, grab Terry's hand, hold it—

She seemed to sense what was happening.

And she ended it—

"Nathan, a lot of time has passed since . . . since we knew each other. We're different people now—"

"Terry, I always wanted to—"

She looked away, and Bridger could see that the pain wasn't really a decade old. It was fresh, not so easily forgotten.

"We both have jobs to do." She looked right at him, the light in her eyes faded now. "And if you let me do my job, then everything will be fine."

"Captain, would you care for some breakfast?" the cook called over to him.

Bridger kept looking at Terry, and then, slowly, he shook his head. And he spoke. "No." He nodded, stood up, and turned to the cook. "No, thanks. I'm not hungry this morning."

As he left, he hoped that Hitchcock and Krieg weren't watching him.

Ernst's briefing was held in Dr. Kristin Westphalen's Science Wing.

Westphalen had already complained to Bridger that Ernst

was being incredibly tight-lipped about what was going on at the Azores base.

"What are they doing down there, Nathan, that they can't tell me?" she asked Bridger, and the Captain had to reassure her that this lack of knowledge was temporary.

"I'm sure you and your science crew will be involved as much as you want to be . . . once we get there."

Then Westphalen, prone to snap decisions, said, "I don't like him."

Bridger almost said, *Nor do I*. But he took a seat while Ernst prepared his downloads from the EarthNet to aid the presentation.

Besides Westphalen, Hitchcock and Ford were there, as well as Terry McShane and Akira Shimura. Bridger would have liked to have had Lucas at the briefing—but already the small conference room was crowded. No matter, Lucas would be able to pick up all the downloads and watch them as they came in . . .

"All set, Dr. Ernst?"

Ernst was hitting the keyboard, downloading images, maps, filmed footage that he wanted to use.

"Er—yes, now . . ." And Ernst turned around. "Thank you all for coming." There was a trace of an accent in his voice, only a slightly Anglicized pronunciation to some words.

Ernst looked a bit better this morning, Bridger saw. Amazing what a good night's sleep could do. "I've been asked by your Captain Bridger to provide a briefing on the hydrothermal vent area we are going to . . ." Ernst smiled, and Bridger saw that the scientist was an old hand at selling his scientific package to groups, probably the big-money boys, the ones who funded the exploratory mining colonies.

There was nothing the mineral and ore wildcatters liked better than a scientist who told them that this square mile on the ocean floor was where they would hit it *big*.

The large paper-thin gas-bubble screen behind Ernst came on, and there was a map of the South Atlantic. The image was 2-D, but the high-definition screen gave it a breathtaking realism. As Ernst talked, the image changed from a satellite photo of the ocean to increasingly tighter views.

"Hydrothermal vents have been places of intense interest on the part of the scientific community ever since their discovery in the 1980s. At that time, a number of oceanographers, including Dr. Robert Ballard—the man who found the *Titanic*—uncovered full-blown ecosystems that developed around the volcanic seeps. These seeps form along fault lines and fissure zones at the ocean's bottom."

The ocean photos gave way to a side view illustration showing the depth of a vent area, and an animated graphic of a submersible going down.

But that sequence was interrupted by filmed footage of the vent creatures—a sight that never failed to impress Bridger. Here were fields of giant tube worms, some stretching twenty feet or more, all tinged with a telltale pinkish color.

Monstrous albino crabs scurried in between the worms, while eyeless shrimps darted around them. Clusters of overgrown mussels dotted the landscape.

"The strange thing about these ecosystems . . ."

Westphalen leaned close to Bridger and whispered, "The way he's talking, you'd think we *weren't* a research ship."

Bridger smiled, nodded, and raised a hand to the chief *seaQuest* scientist. "Let him go on. I want to see where he ends up with all this."

". . . was that they were essentially *alien* systems. The creatures that lived in the vent areas didn't depend on the photosynthetic cycle of the surface. There, in the abyssal blackness, they had developed a life cycle that depended on chemosynthesis."

That was truly incredible, Bridger thought. Somehow the tube worms had developed an ability to take the poisonous hydrogen sulfides, a toxin, and turn them into food. And how they did it was even more bizarre.

"Adding interest to these life forms is the symbiotic relationship between the tube worms, the primary producer of food, and the bacteria that live inside the host worms."

There were close-up images of the worms, flowing gently in the deep-ocean current, followed by lab footage of a pulpy-white worm being dissected, via robotic manipulator arms, in a tank under high pressure—guaranteeing that the tissue material wouldn't disintegrate.

"The tube worms depend on a bacterial parasite, a colony creature living inside them, to survive. The parasite takes the toxin and makes food for the worm, while the worm allows the bacteria to live.

"One big happy family," Bridger wisecracked.

Everyone in the room—excepting Ernst—laughed. And like a chagrined schoolteacher, Ernst waited until he had the attention of his audience.

"Shall I proceed, Captain?"

"Oh, yes—sorry. It's only that most of us have a pretty thorough grounding in the life cycle of the vent creatures. We're waiting for you to get to the point."

Just then, Ernst smiled. And Bridger felt that, yes, there was someplace that Ernst was going with this . . .

Bridger wondered what it might mean to his ship.

Noyce couldn't sleep. He got up and sat on the edge of his bed, staring into the darkness of his stylish brownstone home, which was within walking distance of Twin Peaks Park.

His wife stirred and sleepily reached out a hand, touching his back.

"Bill . . . what's wrong?"

He shook his head in the darkness. "Nothing," he said. Then, fabricating, he added, "A headache."

He stood up and started to maneuver through the dark room. "I'm going to get a Tylenol . . ."

His wife grunted, already falling back to sleep, the alarm over.

Noyce walked out of the bedroom and shut the door gently behind him. He turned on the hallway light, the brilliant glass of the fixture so sparkling and bright it hurt his eyes.

He walked to the bathroom.

Now his head did throb. *Maybe I will take something,* he thought, *splash some water on my face . . .*

He entered the bathroom, gently touched a panel, and the light came on. He studied himself in the mirror.

He looked at his grizzled face, the day's growth of beard so gray. *I look like a homeless person,* he thought. He turned on the cold water and then scooped up a double handful of San Francisco's best tap water.

Noyce splashed the water onto his face, and he was even more awake. He looked like he'd been out in the rain, or sweating, or crying, and—

Then he knew what had awakened him.

It's guilt, he thought.

Guilt that he hadn't told Nathan Bridger the whole story, that he had had to leave certain things out . . . for now.

Had to do it, he thought.

Had to.

Didn't I?

Would Bridger ever forgive him?

As long as he was up, Noyce decided to take a shower, get dressed, maybe call for his car early.

After all, he wanted to be with *seaQuest* every step of the way on this one . . . even if Nathan Hale Bridger never knew it . . .

"The Azores field was discovered in 2016 by a joint team operating under the auspices of IFREMER, the French Oceanographic Institute, and the UEO."

There was nothing on the HD screens. All eyes were on Ernst, and he seemed to like it that way.

Guy knows how to hold someone's attention, Bridger thought.

"It was the largest field ever discovered, nearly thirty acres. And it was also the one with the most complicated topography. There were dozens of 'black smokers,' the giant spouts pouring out superheated water hot enough to melt the viewport of a submersible. There were caves, and canyons, and nasty volcanic ridges, and—everywhere—living things."

"Tell us something we don't know," Westphalen whispered. Bridger looked at her. She had done her own extensive work with the chemosynthesizers of the vents.

Ernst's face was set.

"What I'm about to tell you has been classified since the discovery of the vent area, kept secret by agreement of IFREMER, the UEO, and the scientific board in charge of the research station that was eventually built there."

Ernst paused. He hit the keyboard connected to the HD screens.

Images came on. More worms, clams, crabs—but there was something different here—the number of them. There was so many, and the colors looked different, the shape—

Westphalen muttered, "My God . . . what—?"

"The life forms found in this vent area were unlike any found in any vent area in the world. They were, like the other vent creatures, a chemosynthetic life form. But this time—they were even *more* alien."

The footage, material that Bridger certainly had never seen before, changed to close-ups, and he saw shellfish with curled bodies, strange shapes, bizarre—

"Beautiful . . . ," Westphalen muttered.

Then Bridger saw a crablike creature scuttle over some of the shellfish. But the crab's body, white and dotted with reddish spots, was unlike anything Bridger had ever seen.

Bridger wondered—Where were the tube worms?

The film, top secret certainly if Westphalen hadn't seen it, moved on, to a giant cliff dotted with burrows, and then there they were . . .

"There was nothing more alien than the worms that were found here . . ."

Closer on the worms, until Bridger felt as if they were in the conference room with them.

And he wanted to get out . . .

CHAPTER 14

Noyce's car sat outside the building, the engine issuing a low purr, waiting for him to come out. His driver, a good-natured Marine named Edison, would wait as long as it took Noyce.

The Admiral liked the city like this, so quiet in the near-dawn, the lights crystalline, the whole effect clean and refreshing.

He sipped his cup of black instant coffee.

When he got to the UEO headquarters over by Fort Wiley and the veteran's hospital, he could get some food if he wanted. Though he couldn't imagine being hungry . . . not today.

He put the cup down on an end table in the living room, grabbed his cap, and left his home.

Outside, there was a tangy, salty smell to the air, the slight taste of the Pacific Ocean sitting at the bottom of the rolling San Francisco hills.

Bill Noyce imagined *seaQuest,* where she was right now, what she looked like cutting through the black water. And he imagined Bridger, irritated, curious, sailing into the unknown . . .

They were tube worms.

But so unlike the worms found at other vent sites—the sleek, smooth-skinned, strange—and harmless—rift worms.

These babies were a whole different story.

"What in the world are they?" Bridger said, voicing the question that everyone watching must have had.

"Good question, Captain. When we first saw them, we thought that they were only a variant of the normal worm colonies but—"

The film took them closer to the field of worms, and at the top of each worm was a clearly visible opening. The opening seemed to be sucking in the water, then blowing it out, sucking it in, blowing it out . . .

Closer . . .

Now Bridger saw that the opening was ringed with what looked like tiny teeth.

"Incredible," Westphalen said. She turned to Bridger. "I must get a look at one of these."

"These are telephoto shots. Our first studies showed us that these worms were not the same as the other worms we've found. As you can see, they are filtering the water, taking in the superheated water, filtering out the toxins. That much *was* similar. But then these worms obviously had teeth, and something that approximated a mouth. Our scientists weren't sure, but—"

And now there was a still, a shot of one of the worms with its mouth open—Dead? Bridger wondered—the teeth plainly visible and a gulletlike opening descending into the center of the worm.

"It looked as if this worm could take sustenance in more ways than the *Riftia pogonophosa Jones* . . ."

Bridger turned to Westphalen, confused. "The name given to the rift worms," the scientist explained.

Ernst nodded. "This was an amazing creature, and there were so many questions. Why was this different creature here? And why were there other strange creatures only at this site? What implications did it have for evolutionary biology? And what could we learn from the creature?"

It was back to action footage now, moving through the vent field, watching the strange crabs scuttle across the field, great garlands of shellfish clustered around the base of the cliff, below the worms.

"Nasty-looking things," Ford said.

Ernst nodded. "Yes, they are, Commander. And what made these creatures even more interesting was that like the normal rift worms, these also consisted of a host and parasite."

"I must see one," Westphalen whispered.

"There is a bacterial parasite inside the worm. And though it's hard to tell, it appears that it is the parasite that controls the worm."

Ralph MacInnis looked at the three people standing in his cramped quarters. The deep-ocean research station had been built quickly, using prefabricated sections originally destined for mining outposts and deep-drilling stations.

Whatever was quick and available—everything was thrown together, everyone was so eager.

MacInnis was sweating. He had told his engineer to jack up the cooling system—and damn, it had to be so cold now. So why was he sweating?

The people—three people he trusted, he *hoped* he could still trust—looked at him.

"MacInnis," the woman said, Dr. Marie Thibaud of IFREMER, "how many hours away is the *seaQuest*?"

Marie too was partially supported by Harpe WorldWide Enterprises. Just about everyone in the station had some connection to Harpe.

MacInnis brushed his brow. "I-I'm not too sure, Marie. Eight . . . ten hours . . ."

"Christ!" Julio Rodriguez, the station engineer, barked out the word. "That's just great, that's *wonderful,* MacInnis. Why didn't you try and get help before—"

Now MacInnis blew. "I *let* them know. You understand? Right away, I *let* them know, but—damn it—there happened to be a terrorist crisis going on."

The other man laughed. He was a balding, round-bellied

man who wore bifocals. He looked as if he should be running a country bookstore.

But he was the person with the closest ties to Harpe Enterprises, the man who'd advise Harpe on the commercial possibilities of whatever was found down here. Morton Dell was the money man, the one who'd tell Harpe and the UEO how much this project could eat up.

"It appears that there's more than a bit of panic in this room." Dell reached into his shirt pocket, removed a pack of cigarettes, and tapped one out. He stuck the cigarette in his mouth and lit it. An expensive and stupid habit . . .

He smokes only to annoy us, MacInnis thought.

"I don't think *anyone's* panicking," MacInnis said. "I've spoken with Mr. Harpe, and with Admiral Noyce."

Dell took a drag on the cigarette. "And you told them everything?" he said with a raised eyebrow.

"No, I told them about the accident—"

Another chuckle from Dell.

"And the importance of getting Dr. Ernst here."

"I'll say—"

Now Rodriguez turned to Dell. "Look, I've had enough of your cracks—"

Dell looked away, but MacInnis saw that he was intimidated by Rodriguez. *I would be too,* MacInnis thought. Rodriguez's temper was a scary thing to see.

"Look," MacInnis interrupted, "Marie, you saw the bodies in the lab. Ernst will want to talk with you right away. And—and, Julio, what areas of the station are sealed? Has there been any attempt—"

Dell stood up. "If I might make a suggestion, Mac. There are still *hours* until *seaQuest* gets here. It may be time that you start handing out weapons . . . to those you can trust."

Dell looked away from Rodriguez, and MacInnis thought the station's engineer was going to go jumping for Dell's throat.

MacInnis licked his lips, tasting his salty sweat. *It's so cold, yet I keep on sweating . . .*

"Right. Sure, weapons. That's a good idea, Dell. Let's do it."

MacInnis led them out of his room, down the long passageway to the locked firearms area.

Ernst shut off the monitor and appeared done with his briefing.

Westphalen looked at Bridger, then the others. "What? Excuse me, Dr. Ernst, but is *that* it?"

Ernst gathered his papers up.

"Yes, Dr. Westphalen?"

"Surely you plan on telling us more—why there's all this urgency in transporting you there, and how your field of paleobiology comes into play?"

Ernst shook his head. "Anything else, I'm afraid, must remain classified. Your captain has been told all that he needs, and I'm afraid I cannot tell you any more of the work being done at the research station."

"This is ridiculous, absolutely—"

"Steady, Kristin. Dr. Ernst"—Bridger looked up at the scientist—"is only doing his job."

Bridger saw Terry McShane get up, and her face looked troubled. There was something about Ernst's presentation that she didn't like. Bridger made a note to talk with Terry later.

Of course, she was playing her own cards pretty close to the vest. This whole expedition was turning into an information sump. And maybe it was time to correct that.

Bridger stood up. "Thank you, Dr. Ernst. Our estimated time of arrival at the station is in a little over seven hours. Now, if you'll excuse me . . ."

Bridger was the first to leave. Because he didn't have a lot of time to get answers to some very difficult questions.

"Busy?" Bridger said, poking his head into Lucas's room.

"Huh? Oh, good afternoon, Captain. I was just downloading some reports on the storm. Mike is kicking butt . . ."

Lucas hit a key, and there appeared a scrawl identifying

the scene as Aruba . . . and Bridger saw a coastline lost to the torrential rain, low clouds, and terrible wind. The giant waves looked as if they were eating the beach.

A quick cut, and there were the streets of Martinique, some buildings collapsed into heaps, others with windows shattered.

"And old Mike's picking up strength, sir."

"Maybe this will teach the Weather Bureau about experimenting with climate alteration."

"Better living through chemistry, sir. The man-made storms were supposed to bring rain to southern California and parts of the Southwest."

Bridger touched Lucas's shoulder. "That they did, but it's like dominoes. Knock one thing over and another falls. And there's a big domino falling today."

Lucas nodded. "I have some footage from Florida, sir. They've started evacuating the Keys, and the mainland's gone on alert. I have some of that, if you'd like to see it . . . Getting ready for the worst storm in a century, they're saying . ."

Bridger looked back at the open door to Lucas's small cabin. He took a step and shut it. He felt Lucas looking at him, wondering what was going on.

"No, Lucas. Not now. Maybe you could save them; I'd like to take a look later. I have a lot of friends on the Gulf Coast." Bridger smiled. "Got one old friend from my days on the destroyer RFK. He lives on Captiva, runs a restaurant called Time Out. Quite a joint . . . Each room is filled with stuff from a different decade—the twenties, the sixties . . ."

Bridger thought of the last time he had been there with Barbara. How they stayed until everyone else was gone, laughing, drinking champagne, and enjoying a spicy conch chowder.

"It's going to be hit hard, Captain. Real hard."

Bridger nodded. "There is something that you can do for me, Lucas . . ."

"Sir?"

Bridger came close, lowering his voice. "I'd like everything you can get on this Dr. Richard Ernst. Where was he trained, what about his specialty . . . and why is it so damned important to get him to that research base? And—"

"Captain, the Net is running slow. There's a lot of heavy emergency use, all the systems being stressed out to the max. Some of them haven't been upgraded since the late nineties."

"Do what you can, Lucas. And find out what you can about this Azores base. Why all this secrecy? See if any hackers out there got anything interesting on what's going on down there."

Lucas took his Marlins hat and turned it around, brim facing back, ready to get to work.

"I'll do my best, sir."

Bridger patted Lucas. "Good—and, Lucas, no need to tell anyone else that I've asked you to do this."

"Yes, sir."

Bridger smiled. Lucas never sounded like a crewperson, even when he said the right words. Lucas was kind of *out there* . . .

Bridger grabbed the handle to let himself out.

He hesitated a moment. "One more thing . . . Could you run a check on Terry McShane. See what you come up with." Bridger smiled, hoping his guilt didn't show. "No biggie."

"I'm on the case, Captain."

The passageway was empty, eerily so, thought MacInnis. Normally, there would have been the hustle and bustle of the station—scientists and technicians walking from the biology lab to the specimen tanks, and dive teams getting ready to head out to the vent field in submersibles.

Now it was quiet, *disturbingly* still.

Their steps echoed eerily on the metal grate of the floor.

All the modules, the work stations of the base, were at the end of the spokes, the long tubular passageways. Offices and smaller labs lined each spoke, and at the central hub there was a large meeting area, the communications center, and the dining facilities for the research station.

Smaller passageways connected the ends of the spokes, linking the major labs and wings of the stations.

But they were closed, locked. God—at least, MacInnis hoped that they were still sealed. Two spokes were sealed off completely—Primary Biology One and the main sub pool.

Everything was contained.

MacInnis hoped.

"Where the hell is everybody?" Rodriguez said.

"Laying low, I imagine," Dell offered.

MacInnis looked at Marie Thibaud. She had come closest to understanding what had happened. An expert in the strange biology of the rift creatures, she had examined the wrecked sub, she had seen the bodies. It was only a miracle that—

They heard steps.

"Finally," Dell said.

MacInnis saw a lone figure standing down at the other end, near the entrance to the hub. The person, a man it appeared, was backlit . . . so it was hard for MacInnis to see who it was.

Instinctively, he stopped walking.

And after a few faltering steps, the others stopped also.

"Hello," MacInnis said. "Who's there . . . ?"

It was silly, as if they were kids, playing a game, hiding from a bully. And MacInnis felt that maybe he should send another report to Harpe or the UEO . . . give them more . . . *information.*

But this fed into his fear. That if they knew *everything,* there was no way in hell they'd let the *seaQuest* come anywhere near the station. Instead, they'd give an order for *seaQuest* to take the station out.

But no, they wouldn't do that. Not with something this important, this *amazing.* MacInnis remembered the look on Harpe's face. There was no fear there, only excitement, tremendous anticipation.

The UEO—well, that could be another story . . .

"Who the hell is it?" Rodriguez said.

None of them moved.

"Hello!" MacInnis said again.

This time the figure, who had been standing still, started to move toward them.

CHAPTER 15

Bridger walked down the sleek passageway that ran through the center of the crew's quarters, and—at the other end— he saw Terry McShane.

On such a big ship, with 280 people on board, it was kind of strange that they would find themselves all alone.

Must be fate, Bridger thought.

"Exploring the ship?" he said.

She smiled. "It's wonderful . . . more like a city."

Bridger grinned. "And it has all the problems of a small city." He paused a second. "Want a tour?"

Terry arched her eyebrows. "Aren't you still convinced that I'm a spy?"

"You may be a spy—but you're a *nice* spy. Besides, we're both working for the same side." He paused a second. "At least, I think that we're working for the same side."

"Thanks, I'd love to see the rest of the *seaQuest*."

"Great. Then, we'll start with Engineering and work our way forward. You know, there are places on board that I've never seen . . ."

Bridger turned around and led Terry aft, wondering,

What's the point of this? To get information from her . . . Or is there something else going on here?

"Absolutely normal vitae." Lucas said to himself, looking at the data on the screen. "Nothing but kaka." He skimmed the text material on Dr. Richard Ernst. There were also icons indicating that there was a photo and monograph files attached, scientific papers delivered by Ernst.

All public stuff.

"No surprises here," Lucas said. He had the material printed out anyway so at least he had something to give the Captain.

"Got to do better than this."

Lucas had an idea how to do it. The *seaQuest*'s mainframe computer was in constant communication with the UEO Net. If Lucas could get clearance to travel that network, he could see what other interesting files were in the secret UEO package.

Even if the files were all tied up with security codes, cracking them should be no problem for him—though there might be some questions later.

The first step was getting into the UEO system—and staying there.

Lucas took his hands and bent them backward, splaying his fingers back, cracking the knuckles.

"Okay, boys and girls," he said, "it's show time."

Dell muttered, "Why don't you just shoot the dumb bas—Oh, I forgot. You don't have a gun yet. What a *pity* . . ."

"Quiet," MacInnis said. "Now, wait a second."

The figure stood very still at the other end of the long passageway, unrecognizable. Marie Thibaud came close to MacInnis, obviously scared.

MacInnis considered turning around and walking back to the pod behind him, back to his office. And do what—hide?

But then the figure, as if on thirty-second delay, said, "Hello? Mr. MacInnis?"

MacInnis nodded, and he felt his breath returning to normal. He identified the voice . . .

"It's Kelly, from Communications. Yeah, that's—"

"You hope it's him . . . ," Dell said.

"Come on," Rodriguez said. "Let's get moving. The longer we stay here . . ."

MacInnis took a step. "Kelly, what is it . . . ?"

Kelly started moving toward them. He had obviously been nervous too, thought MacInnis. That standing, waiting . . . He had been scared too. Makes sense . . .

"Mr. MacInnis, there's something wrong over at Bio One."

"Let's get those guns, eh, gang?" Dell said.

"Wrong?"

"All the sensor readings from the sealed passageways have been cut. There's interference of some kind, I don't know—it's like the computer can't see into those pods anymore."

"Isn't that swell," Dell said.

MacInnis turned to him. "Will you shut up? Just shut up." And MacInnis wanted to take a swing at the sarcastic bastard.

Dell put up his hands. "Sorry, just trying to inject a bit of levity into the situation."

MacInnis turned his attention back to Kelly as the communications person walked beside him. "So, we're blind in there?"

MacInnis's stomach was tight, as if he could throw up. And he hadn't had any food in twelve hours.

"Completely blind, sir. I could try to organize a tech team to go in." Now Kelly grinned. "But I don't think we'd get any volunteers, sir. It would have to be an order. And even then—"

MacInnis felt like groaning. "Any word from *seaQuest*?"

"They're making steady progress toward our position. They can't be more than three, maybe four hours away."

"Let's go," MacInnis said, and he led his group to the central pod, the communications and research hub of the base. And MacInnis saw the various teams—the EVA people, the submersible team, the various scientists and research people—standing around.

It looked like the saddest birthday party ever.

Who forgot the party hats?

They were waiting for words of wisdom.

And I have none, MacInnis thought.

There's no way he could make a team go into the sealed wings. Not without putting a gun to someone's head. Absolutely impossible.

His mind racing, MacInnis thought about what he should do. Guard the points of entrance, get weapons to everyone he could trust, and—?

"Mac . . ." It was Marie Thibaud.

"Yes, Marie?"

"What happens . . . when the *seaQuest* gets here, and they learn what's happening, what's really going on? There's no way they'll come in."

Dell laughed. *"There's* a bright girl."

MacInnis raised his hands. "No." He spun around the room, aware that everyone was watching him. "They can be ordered in . . ." He took a breath. "They will be ordered to come in."

Rodriguez came close to him. "Let's get those guns out, MacInnis."

MacInnis nodded, wondering what was going on in the two sealed-off spokes of the research station, feeling as if *he* were the one trapped.

Katherine Hitchcock looked up from a long table that displayed all the data about the ship's current running performance.

"Oh, Captain, I didn't see you. Is there a problem?"

"No, Hitchcock, I'm only showing off the wonders of the *seaQuest.*"

And wonders they were, even to Bridger. This large main engineering room was the heart of the sub. Here the nuclear fusion-powered turbines were monitored, the power output constantly adjusted to meet the demands of the rest of the ship. This was also the control center for the air, water, and waste systems.

It was all self-running and self-monitoring—so the engineers said—but without Hitchcock watching over it, Bridger doubted he'd feel too comfortable a mile or two under the water.

"Where are the fusion reactors?" Terry said.

"Just below us," Hitchcock answered. "He's a powerful ship—but a quiet one."

"He?"

Bridger smiled as he explained. "Hitchcock insists on seeing *seaQuest* as a male."

Now it was Hitchcock's turn to laugh. "Have you seen the shape of this vessel, Captain? I'm from the ranch country of Wyoming, and, well, if this ship isn't a male, then I've got my biology all wrong."

Terry laughed, and Bridger found that a wonderful sound. Everything had been so serious in his life lately, Bridger thought, trying to lose himself in his work. Lose himself . . . and forget Barbara.

Laughter was such a wonderful thing.

"Well, how about the moon pool—you saw it briefly when you came in, but it's quite an amazing place."

"Lead on."

"I'm in," Lucas whispered. "*Crystal.* Inside the UEO Net. Now to—"

He reached for a handful of M&Ms. "Energy pellets," he called them when he spent too many hours at the console and stopping to eat was a luxury he couldn't afford.

"Now, to break whatever ICE they're using."

ICE—Intrusion Countermeasure Electronics—could vary from system to system, Lucas knew. It could range from only token resistance to something vicious that could travel back to the probing computer system and make it crash. As a precaution, Lucas had isolated his own terminal from *seaQuest*—so the ship's systems were protected.

Unless they had some really special ICE, really new, Lucas felt he should be able to get in and out without catching too much electronic flak.

He sat back while his computer tried access codes, trying the millions of permutations, testing possibilities, as the numbers fell into place.

"Bingo!" Lucas said, as the code locked in. As he passed through the first gateway, it didn't appear that any alarms were going off—

There was a knock at the door. Lieutenant Krieg opened it and stuck his head in.

"Hey, Wolenczak—gaming night tonight. Be there or—"

Lucas waved him away.

"Hey, what are you doing, bud?"

"Shut the door," Lucas said. "And don't let it hit you on the way out." Krieg shrugged and left.

Lucas watched the screen display the initial UEO menu. From here, the system would be wide open—or maybe not, but at least Lucas could see what they had.

"Okay, let's look at—"

He clicked on the raised letters that said, "Scientific Files." For a moment, the word "processing" flashed.

Still no trouble.

Then, there was the main directory.

Only a mere 560 pages long! And that was only the table of contents.

Lucas popped more M&Ms.

"There's *got* to be a search procedure," he said. He tried a few possibilities, different combinations of what he hoped were hot keys, worrying that the system might only be accessed by voice at this level.

Which would end the game right here.

But then he tapped one of the function buttons, and got a submenu. And one of the items offered for his dining enjoyment was . . . "*Search*."

"There we go," he said. "I wonder if I can put in a string request . . . link Ernst, the Azores . . . and see what I get."

He hit the keys. This part of the system was moving fast. Not much traffic, he guessed. He put in his search words, thinking this was almost too easy . . .

When the screen turned red.

Two words appeared at the bottom.

"*Security alert.*"

Uh-oh. Bad news, Lucas thought. The security alert identified him as a possible intruder.

He had only a few seconds to convince the system that he belonged there, or he'd be shut out—probably for good.

Lucas pulled his chair close, riding his rocket, hitting the keys like crazy—a network cowboy riding one nasty pony . . .

By the time Admiral Noyce got to his UEO office, the sun was at the horizon.

The rest of the world was coming awake now, he thought. And it felt as if the few moments of being alone, to think, had vanished . . .

He decided to contact Bridger. Tell him what he hadn't told him before, that the research base was actually a joint project of Harpe WorldWide and the UEO.

He should have told him that before, he thought. Come clean . . . but if he had, what would Bridger have done?

Or rather—what would Bridger *not* have done?

The UEO had let Harpe get involved in the Azores station because he had the experts needed—and Harpe offered the cash to finance what would be a costly, secret operation.

Now there was something very wrong there.

There was a knock at Noyce's door.

"Admiral, Mr. Harpe wishes to speak with you."

Noyce looked up at his screen. *How does he know I'm here?* Noyce wondered.

Noyce nodded and said, "Put him through—and as soon as we're done, put me through to the *seaQuest*."

"Yes, sir."

It was time to put all the cards on the table.

"The moon pool can accommodate the full component of submersibles and minisubs that the *seaQuest* holds, everything from the two-person speeders to the deep-ocean transport berthed over—"

The Captain stopped talking.

Bridger hadn't been looking at the pool when they entered the launch area. And he certainly hadn't seen Lianna Hays, the EarthNet reporter, standing at one end while a HoloCam operator filmed her.

"Wait a second—what the hell are you doing?"

Bridger hurried over to the EarthNet reporter while McShane followed.

"Captain Bridger, you just ruined that take."

"Terribly sorry, but I don't remember giving you permission to—"

"Captain—" Hays was a striking woman, and now—for an actual taping—she looked more stunning than normal, her black hair falling in luxurious waves, framing her dark skin and eyes.

Bridger had been forced to let her aboard, to let her document the "wonder of the *seaQuest*" for regular EarthNet consumption. PR and budget approval, they went hand in hand.

"Unless I'm wrong, this is my ship and this is a secure area."

Hays smiled condescendingly. "Your executive officer, Commander Ford, approved this."

Bridger would have to talk with Ford later—though Ford had probably assumed that Hays had been given free rein to film.

"And what exactly are you doing here?"

"I'm reporting on the SousMer incident, Captain. There's a special report about it on all the news feeds tonight." Hays smiled. "You may find yourself a hero, Captain."

He caught Hays looking at Terry McShane, and not in a friendly way. Bridger introduced her. "Oh—this is Terry McShane, with the UEO."

Hays, ever gracious, extended a hand. "How nice to meet you. And you were in the resort?"

"Why, yes—I was—"

Bridger took a step backward.

"Maybe she'll find out what you were doing there," Bridger muttered to Terry.

He took another step away.

"I imagine Ms. Hays will want to get a holo of you for the big show. We'll pick up the rest of the tour . . ." Bridger kept backing up, while Terry gave him a look as if saying, *Don't abandon me*. ". . . later."

The *seaQuest* was getting close to the research station, and it was time Bridger checked on the arrival, thinking that maybe—after this—a week of R&R in San Francisco wouldn't be such a bad idea.

Lucas jumped back from the keyboard.

The warning stopped flashing, and then it disappeared completely.

"Did I do it?" Lucas said. Then adopting the voice of Tweety Bird he said, "Yes, I think I certainly dood it. That wasn't too tough," he said, referring to the ICE. "Not tough at all."

He entered the command to search—under *Dr. Richard Ernst, Azores Deep-Sea Research Station,* and, remembering the Captain's other question, *Terry McShane.*

He sat back, watched, and then the data started coming in—

He stood up.

"Man, give me a break. Give me a—"

He speed-read the data as it flew by on the screen, while it instantaneously printed out behind him.

He leaned close to the screen. "Can you say 'bad news,' boy and girls?"

And then the top-secret download got even more interesting, when the system started scouring Terry McShane's file.

CHAPTER 16

"Mr. Ortiz, are you in contact with the station?"

"Yes, Captain. They just now uploaded some revisions to the topo file for that part of the seafloor."

Bridger settled into his command chair. His hand brushed against the targeting and fire console on the right arm. They were all inactive now, but the feel of them—so close—reminded Bridger of the tremendous firepower that the *seaQuest* carried.

"Sir," Ortiz said, "do you want the updated topo on the VR screen or—?"

"No, Lieutenant. Can you project a holo image overhead?"

There was a brief pause, and then a chunk of the ocean floor was suspended in front of Bridger, looking as if he could reach out and touch it.

"Mr. Ortiz, where's the station?"

"Captain, since the station has been classified, we don't have its layout. But they have told us their coordinates . . . which I can highlight—"

And then one of the folds in the craggy, uncompromising vent area was highlighted in red.

"And where is the vent field?"

"In that valley, sir. It opens to a field of volcanic chimneys, sir."

The section behind the resort area also became tinged in red.

Bridger had two thoughts:

First, this was one *hell* of a big vent area. The largest vent area he had heard about was only ten acres, and this one had to be easily three, four times that size.

And his second thought was that they couldn't have picked a more difficult area for the *seaQuest* to operate in. The station looked as if it were hidden in the rocky folds of the seafloor. It was surrounded by nasty sharp-edged volcanic ridges, mountains, and jagged, upthrust points of rock.

The *seaQuest* was no little ship. It would take some careful navigating . . .

"Doesn't look too pretty, eh, Captain?"

Chief Crocker came up beside Bridger.

Bridger looked down from the holographic image of the topo. "No, Gator. In fact, I can't remember seeing such a nasty area."

Crocker leaned close to the Captain, as if he didn't want anyone else on the bridge to hear.

"Excuse me for saying so, Captain, but while the ship's still pretty new to you—well, I'd take it real easy."

Bridger laughed. "Don't worry, Crocker. I'm not about to bang up the UEO's pride and joy."

"Aye, aye, sir."

"But—I do think I'd better get her down, and approach this"—he looked at the topo—"mess level on."

Ford stood by the communications module, talking to Bachmann. "Mr. Ford. Let's bring *seaQuest* down a bit."

Ford turned to Bridger. "Sir?"

"Blow forward and rear ballast, and trim forward dive planes to take her down 30 degrees, Mr. Ford."

In less than a second, Navigation started carrying out his orders, and Bridger knew that this massive ship, this underwater city, was swimming deeper now, cutting farther into the blackness of the deep ocean.

He barely felt the tilt set by the dive planes.

"Captain," Ford said, "I'll check the currents. There's a lot of strange stuff kicked up by the storm."

Bridger nodded. "Good idea, and Mr. Ortiz? Deploy WSKRS, and see that—"

"Captain—" Bridger heard a yell, and then steps from behind, someone running from the starboard passageway. He spun around in his chair to see Lucas running toward him with a sheaf of papers in his hands.

"Captain—whoa, you better take a look at these."

Bridger looked up to see everyone on the bridge watching him, curious—everyone a little on edge, not knowing what this was all about.

"As you were, gentlemen," and Bridger took the hard copy from Lucas.

Noyce studied Harpe's face on the screen just as he was sure Harpe was studying his.

Bill Noyce had been brought into this party with the joint UEO/Azores station a "done deal"—the vent field already discovered and Harpe backing research, in exchange for certain proprietary rights.

Now Noyce wanted to know exactly what those rights were.

"Mr. Harpe, I had expected to hear from you about my previous requests."

Harpe looked stolid, unflappable. "Requests? You mean, Admiral, about the timetable of events at the station? I'm afraid—"

Noyce had received some direct reports from the station, but the UEO's communications people told him that a steady stream of two-way contact had been going back and forth between the station and Harpe WorldWide.

"Mr. Harpe—what exactly happened to that sub?"

Wrecked, its two-man crew dead. That's all Noyce knew.

Harpe smiled. "I'm afraid that's the million-dollar question, Admiral. In fact, that's why it's so good that your *seaQuest* is sailing there right now. My people . . ."

Noyce shook his head. How the hell had they gotten into bed with this lizard?

". . . haven't had the opportunity to examine the sub." Harpe looked irritated by the question. "With over a half dozen people dead, Admiral, and—who knows—more on the way, surviving has been their number one priority."

Noyce cleared his throat. Enough of this. "Harpe, as of now, I want all communications with the station to go through the UEO's link. And that also means communications from any HW employees at the station—"

Harpe shook his head. "Admiral, are you ordering me—?"

"I'm *telling* you that there will be no more private communications between you and the Azores station. Everything—all messages, all contact—goes through UEO headquarters starting now. And it will remain that way until we know what happened."

Harpe looked as if he were going to explode out of his seat, but then—after a beat—a composed smile returned to his face.

"Certainly, Admiral Noyce. Whatever you say is best." He paused. "My only interest is the safety of the people at the station."

Noyce, who had girded himself to battle Harpe, felt as if he had been suddenly left swinging at the wind.

It had been too easy, he thought. Much too easy . . .

Something wasn't right. But for the moment, Noyce didn't have a clue what it could be.

Geoffrey Harpe sat perfectly still for a moment. The way Noyce had spoken to him made Harpe want to smash something, perhaps pick up one of his clay statues from the Malay Peninsula—a priceless work a thousand years old—and throw it to the marble floor.

He sat for a second, breathing steadily, calming himself.

Then he spoke to his own faceless communications network, which had been monitoring the audio and the visual contact with Noyce.

"Was that enough?" Harpe said.

"Computer imaging reports that it was plenty, Mr. Harpe. They're working on the program now."

Harpe nodded. "And they got enough . . ." He waved his hand—what was the word? ". . . sibilants, blends, whatever—?"

"Mr. Harpe, the initial check shows that they have everything needed, and it should be ready to run . . ."

C'mon, c'mon, c'mon, Harpe thought, *don't disappoint me.*

". . . in one hour."

Harpe smiled. That was plenty of time.

A few minutes ago Noyce had been acting the big boss. *And in one hour, he'll be my puppet,* Harpe thought gleefully.

Ah, the wonders of modern living.

"Do you mind if we HoloVid this?" Lianna Hays said, as if it were only a formality. Her camera operator, in T-shirt and dungarees, was chewing gum, and Terry saw that he was already taping.

Terry thought of saying no. *No, I don't want to have my face flashed on the EarthNet news feeds, translated into sixty-odd languages, downloaded into a couple of million private data bases, the words cut, sliced, trimmed, examined . . .*

Anyone with a decent voice stress analysis device would be able to know that she was lying.

But if she refused to cooperate, well then they'd *know* that she was hiding something.

"Is this a live feed?" Terry asked.

Lianna Hays smiled, her face expressing shock. "Oh, no. This will be uploaded later."

Terry chewed her lip. "Can I get a look at it . . . before you send it out?"

Lianna raised her eyes. "Look at it?"

"Only to check if I say anything that might embarrass the UEO." She had a brainstorm. "It wouldn't look good for you if something I said unguardedly went out over the Net, something that threatened security."

Lianna smiled, a professional recognizing a well-played move. "Why certainly. Jim can let you check the footage when we're done. Now then . . ."

Terry took a breath.

Hays faced the camera. "I'm talking with Ms. Terry McShane of the UEO. Ms. McShane is one of the heroes of the terrorist threat to the resort." Then Hays turned to Terry. "Ms. McShane, it was certainly lucky that you were at SousMer when this terrible thing occurred. Can you tell us what exactly you were doing there?"

Terry licked her lips. *Let's try not to look too guilty here.* "I, er, was having a short vacation before returning to my duties at UEO headquarters."

Terry looked away from Hays and right over at the camera. She thought that she could feel it zooming in, probing, an insistent, cool, objective eye that could read her like a book.

"How convenient," Hays said. "I thought that the resort was only for the most wealthy . . . I guess"—now Hays looked out at the camera, her smirk as big and broad as she could make it—"I was wrong."

Then she turned back to Terry. "You weren't the guest of anyone, someone else at the resort . . . ?"

Terry shook her head. *No, your Honor, I wasn't.*

Terry relaxed a bit, seeing where Hays was going with this. She was looking for an illicit affair, a wealthy, well-placed paramour. Maybe it would be good to lead her down that road.

Terry shook her head coyly. "I was on vacation . . ."

Akira Shimura held up an electronic syringe. The digital readout told him how many cc's of the antibiotic were in the thin, gunlike barrel.

He caught Darwin looking up at him.

"More medicine, yes, Darwin. But you are getting better. And soon, I can put your communication unit back. You'd like that?"

Darwin shifted in the tank. He was eager, Shimura thought, excited at the thought of talking again.

Or—

Shimura looked at one of the dolphin's eyes, which appeared wide, desperate. And Shimura stopped.

"What is it, Darwin?" Something was bothering the dolphin. But what could it be? Was it pain? Was Darwin in pain? Had he missed something?

Then Shimura got this terrible feeling that Darwin knew something, that Darwin was—

He looked at that eye, so large and expressive—

Darwin was scared.

Shimura brought the electronic syringe down and quickly injected the dolphin. Then Shimura used his good hand to brush Darwin's skin, stroking it, soothing it . . .

"Soon, Darwin. Soon I'll let you talk again. I want to be sure there's no chance of infection." He ran his hand from the dolphin's great bulb-shaped head back to the tail fin. "Soon," Shimura cooed . . .

Darwin looked as if he couldn't wait.

Bridger looked up at Lucas.

"How did you get this? No—don't answer that. It's probably better if I *don't* know. Unfortunately, I don't have a clue what to do with this"—the Captain rattled the papers—"stuff."

Bridger got out of the command chair. "First, I want to show it to Westphalen. And can you get back on-line and keep digging? Who knows? You might get lucky."

"My machine's still digging even as we speak, Captain."

"Great." Bridger started toward the aft elevator, heading down to Westphalen's lab. But then he stopped quickly and turned.

"You did good, kid."

"It must have been terrifying, Ms. McShane, facing those terrorists in the resort's dive area. Can you tell us what that was like?"

"Actually, Commander Ford was the one who cornered them. I only tried to help."

Hays grimaced slightly, and Terry saw that she wasn't happy with the answer. But—so far, so good—no terribly embarrassing moments. And she had to be done soon.

"Yes—well, I'm sure Commander Ford will also give you a lot of the credit. But I'd like to ask one last question."

Terry relaxed. The ordeal was almost over.

"What exactly are you here for, on the *seaQuest*?"

McShane took a breath.

She nodded her head, and smiled. Then, very evenly, she said, "I'm afraid I can't answer that question because of security reasons—other than to say that it's a routine part of my job."

Lianna Hays tilted her head and made a moue of disappointment. "Oh, that's too bad. Then"—Hays turned and looked at the camera—"I guess we'll all have to speculate, won't we?"

Hays waited a beat and then said, "Cut."

She extended her hand to McShane. "Why, thank you for—"

But McShane brushed past her, imagining how the interview would play out on the nightly news.

Kristin Westphalen shuffled through the papers that Bridger had handed her. She shook her head, and then started shuffling through them again.

Finally, she looked up at Bridger. "What is this, Captain Bridger, some kind of joke?"

"I don't think that they were meant to be seen by anyone not inside the UEO."

Bridger wasn't surprised that Westphalen was impressed. The pages detailed the amazing history of the research station—and an even more amazing future.

Now Bridger wanted Westphalen to explain to him what it all meant as they got closer to the station.

"Educate me," Bridger said.

"Okay—see this here." Westphalen pointed to the first page of the dense printout. "That's material we already know, the location of the hydrothermal vent site, the variations in the creatures, nothing too extraordinary there. But look down here."

Bridger nodded. He knew what Westphalen was pointing at.

"This is a reference to a report on the body chemistry of the new worms, now dubbed *Riftia pogonophosa Azores*. Someone obviously got one of these new worms on board—dead it seems—and then took it apart."

"And—?"

"Don't play dumb with me, Captain. I know your work on the island with the biochemistry of coral groups and ocean-borne bacteria. I read your monograph on red tide."

"The folks at Nature didn't like it. They tore it apart."

"Yes, professional jealousy, I suspect. But it was quite good. So, you know what this means? This new worm, like the other tube worms, is locked in a symbiotic relationship with a bacterial parasite. Only in this case, the bacterial colony *completely* controls the creature. God, according to this analysis, it can even use the creature to obtain what it needs for nutrition, whether the hydrogen sulfide toxins, or—"

Bridger nodded. The implication of the report was clear. "They seem to say that the bacterial colony could live in other creatures, could get nutrients from—"

Westphalen nodded. "Yes, *anything* alive. Anything at all. You know, if someone had asked me, I would have said that the area should have been quarantined. Without knowing more, this could be one *very* dangerous organism. Something has kept it locked in that trench, a bizarre biological variant left over from the first million years of evolution perhaps—and now we're going to give it a second crack at existing on the planet?"

Westphalen flipped to the next page. "Look. Here. There were even warning signs. They experimented with the bacterial colony, the colony creature that controlled the worm. God, they should have seen that it posed a great threat."

Bridger took a breath. "I suspect commercial interests dominated the decisions. Look at the next page."

Westphalen laughed and read the name. "Harpe World-

153

Wide Enterprises." The scientist looked up. "Makes sense. Sure, it would be a heavy expenditure for the UEO by itself. Especially for a top secret, fully equipped deep-sea research station. Harpe made it all possible."

"Harpe hoped to gain something out of the deal."

"Oh, you're only too right there, Nathan. A creature like this could be the ultimate biological weapon. If the UEO didn't want to develop it, I bet they were scared enough to learn what could stop it if someone else did."

"And Harpe?"

"If he wasn't out to sell the biotechnology of the creature, you can be sure that he'd get all the information, and the commercial uses. Perhaps in industry, in destroying toxic waste, in medical research. There certainly could be big money in this . . ."

"Enter Dr. Richard Ernst?"

"Well, yes, I bet he's being brought down to take over the project."

"A paleobiologist?"

"Well, you can see, that's only one of his specialties. But on this case, it makes sense. What they're dealing with is a primitive, violent form of life. It's an alien biology, Nathan. If someone can help them . . . control it, it would be Ernst."

Bridger made a mental note to talk to Ernst. The time for charades was over.

Westphalen looked at other sheets of paper in Bridger's hand. "What are those, Captain?"

Bridger shook his head. "Nothing. I had Lucas do a check on Terry McShane." He paused—and then lied. "It's nothing . . ."

Bridger's mind was racing with what he had to do. Contact Noyce, confront him? Find out what the status of the station was, and—talk to McShane.

But there was one more question for Westphalen.

"Kristin, tell me. Your best guess. What's going on down there? What is Ernst's role?"

Bridger wanted to add, *and what the hell should I do?*

Westphalen paused, looked at the pages again.

"Best guess? Well, Nathan, I'd say they've got a problem down there, a problem that they hope Dr. Richard Ernst can help them with." She looked right at Bridger. "What if one of these things got loose? Bet that would turn the station into a madhouse, panic in the streets—out of control."

Westphalen handed the pages back to Bridger. "After all, Captain, imagine if one of those worms got into *seaQuest*. Imagine what that would be like . . ."

That was something Bridger had already imagined.

CHAPTER 17

MacInnis unfastened the electronic combination lock to the cabinet holding the weapons. A light on the keypad blinked green, and MacInnis quickly opened the door. He pulled out three electron-mag hand weapons.

"That's all?" Dell said.

"There are some standard firearms," MacInnis said. "I-I'll get those out too."

"Good idea," Dell snorted.

MacInnis handed one of the electron-mag weapons to Dell, one to Marie Thibaud, and the other to Rodriguez.

"I've never fired one of these," Marie said.

"No problem, my dear. Only make sure that the targeting tracer is on." Dell leaned close to Thibaud. "Throw the switch thusly, and you should be all set. A slight squeeze, and you'll get a tracer beam. Pick up your target, pull the trigger, and bang!"

"Take out some of the other guns," Rodriguez said.

MacInnis nodded and pulled out a few handguns and a box of shells.

Dell looked up. "Just be careful who you give them to, eh?"

Thibaud looked nervous. Maybe, MacInnis thought, that's because she's the only one who really understands what we're up against.

"Okay, we're armed. Everyone stay calm," MacInnis said. "Let's get to the communications center and see how far away the *SeaQuest* is."

"While we hold down the fort . . . ," Dell said.

The group followed MacInnis out of the locked supply room and walked toward the center of the station.

"Where's Admiral Noyce?" Bridger asked Bachmann.

"I don't know, sir. I show that we're linked up, linked to UEO headquarters. We should be through to—"

Noyce's assistant, Captain Gerry Wilson, appeared on the screen. Wilson was smiling with all the sincerity of a hungry wolverine, Bridger thought.

"Captain—" Wilson said. "We didn't expect you to contact us until you reached the station."

"Put Admiral Noyce through," Bridger said testily.

"I'm afraid that the Admiral is busy right now. If you have a question . . ."

Bridger felt as if he might jump out of his seat.

"Put the Admiral through now, damn it, or I'll stop the *seaQuest* and turn back. And you've got two minutes before I give that order."

Wilson's face took on a sick expression. Good, thought Bridger. He was eager to confront the Admiral and ask him why he had lied.

Everyone on the bridge was going about their jobs—Crocker, Ford, Ortiz—but Bridger knew that they all had their eyes and ears cocked for what was going to happen.

And then Noyce was there, looking every bit as discomfited as Bridger had imagined he would.

"Admiral—I've just learned some interesting information about the Azores station."

Noyce shifted in his seat. No gallon of ice cream was going to bail the Admiral out this time. Sucker me once, shame on you. Sucker me twice—

"What's that, Captain?"

He was aware that this was being watched, thought Bridger.

"Does the name Geoffrey Harpe mean anything to you, Admiral? Geoffrey Harpe, Harpe WorldWide Enterprises?"

Noyce shook his head. "So you know about the station. Who got that information for you—Lucas? He should know—"

Bridger leaned forward in his chair. "Why didn't you tell me that Harpe was involved?"

Noyce shook his head. "Because . . . because if I told you, then I could be damn sure of one thing, Nathan."

"Which is?"

"That you'd want to have nothing to do with taking Dr. Ernst there."

Bridger nodded. The Admiral was most assuredly right. But now there was another card to be played.

"And how come you didn't tell us anything about what's really going on there?"

"What do you mean?"

"The worms, Admiral. These new worms. Something damned strange is going on at the station."

Now it was Noyce's turn to lean forward. "Nathan, can we go private on this?"

Bridger looked over at Bachmann. The Captain leaned down and picked up his VR goggles from the side of his chair. "Okay, Mr. Bachmann."

The words "private communication" flashed inside the goggles.

"It's just between us now, Bill."

"I knew, Nathan . . ." Noyce took a breath. "I knew that if I told you that the Azores station was a joint project of Harpe and the UEO, you'd want no part of it."

"Go on . . ."

"And it was vital to get Ernst to the station . . . except I didn't know how vital."

"I don't understand."

"In the time since you picked up Ernst, something has happened in the station. There's been an incident involving a minisub. Some station crew were killed. We're still

159

trying to get a handle on what's happening."

"How could you get into bed with a predator like Harpe?"

"I didn't 'get into bed' with him. The scientific board was strapped for capital to construct a large deep-sea station. Harpe's research division was interested in spin-offs. It was a 'done deal' by the time I came aboard as the UEO director."

Bridger waited, letting Noyce stew. This was a crossroads, Bridger knew. If Noyce didn't tell him something this time, it could happen again.

"Er, how's Darwin?"

"Much better. He should have his communication rig back on in a few hours."

"Good, I'm glad—"

"Admiral, what are we heading into?"

Noyce licked his lips. "That's just it, Nathan. We don't have a clue. We're getting reports from the station, and Harpe has communicated with some of his employees. But—near as we can figure it—one of the worms was brought in—"

"Alive?"

Noyce nodded. "Alive, and—we don't know—it killed someone."

Bridger looked away. In other words. he thought, the situation was a disaster. And he was only learning about it now . . .

"Nathan, what are you going to do?"

Bridger laughed. What could he do, resign his commission? The paperwork was barely done. He looked right at his old friend Bill Noyce.

"What do you think I'm going to do, Bill? I'm going to finish my job. And we can talk about this later."

"Good, I was—"

"But I want everything you have on the station, the life forms at the event. Double-check everything Lucas has to see if there's anything else we should know."

"You got it."

"And Bill—"

"Yes?"

"Next time, don't lie to me."

Bridger pulled off his goggles. "Mr. Bachmann, alert Lucas that we'll be getting a download from UEO."

"Yes, sir."

"Captain," Ortiz said through the intercom. "We're thirty minutes cruising time from the Azores station. I've got some WSKRS data coming in."

"Mr. Ford, keep a watch on what Junior and Mother pick up. And how about a live cam shot on VR number two? Oh, and ask Dr. Ernst and Terry McShane to come to the conference room."

Bridger slid out of his chair. "Let's learn as much as we can before we enter the hot zone."

"Aye, aye, sir," Ford said, and Bridger walked off the bridge with a sick feeling growing in his gut.

The unknown, that's what this feeling was, Bridger thought. The unknown . . . and—maybe—the dangerous.

Rafael Vargas, lying on the bunk in his cabin, listened to the hum of the Skipjack's engines.

His cabin was the same size, the same dimensions, as that of any other crewman on the modified ship.

But there had been many modifications to the ship. Vargas's Skipjack—*El Muerto*—was fitted with a trio of hydrogen turbines that powered two giant silent screws that could move the Skipjack almost as fast as the *seaQuest* itself.

While not armed with nuclear weapons—that would be too risky, too easily detected by satellite surveillance—the Skipjack was modified with additional torpedo tubes fore and aft.

There were also laser guns mounted on the deck, and an enlarged access bay for launching minisubs—the two-man attack subs that were also armed to the teeth.

There were other subs with more power . . .

Still, it was early in Vargas's career.

Vargas thought of Mary Knox. Though he couldn't say he loved her—how could you love someone that dangerous, that deadly?—still he would miss her. Miss her golden hair, her porcelain skin, her intelligence, and her terrible cool.

Grace under pressure.

With Bloody Mary dead, there would be a hole in the Vargas organization, a hole that would be hard to fix. But not, he thought, hard to revenge.

The blame was easy to place. Captain Nathan Hale Bridger and his *seaQuest* must die. And it must happen soon.

Vargas smiled at the thought. And yes, Mary Knox would like that idea too, the giant flagship sub of the UEO destroyed, its three hundred people gone. And there would be no ransom money asked.

This act would be non-negotiable. Sudden, terrible . . . vicious.

An old-fashioned hit.

It was a long trip to the South Atlantic, to where the *seaQuest* sailed.

But there will be no hiding for you, Captain Bridger, Rafael thought. *No hiding from* El Muerto.

No hiding from your own rendezvous with death.

"Now, listen up. Listen up, damn it."

The assorted station crew were gathered in the communications pod. MacInnis saw the fear in their eyes.

"The *seaQuest* is only minutes away, and they'll get us out of here. But we have to keep our cool, and—"

One man, a computer technician, yelled out, "What if they don't come here? What if they stop? What if they want to know what's going on?"

The crowd started murmuring at that, a nasty sea of anxiety and fear that threatened to go out of control.

"They'll *come*. But we can't scare them, scare the UEO. We've got the problem solved, contained . . ."

"But that's not true!" It was another man, one of the submersible engineers. "Sure, those two spokes are closed off—"

"Yes, and no one can—"

"But they've already linked up, they're going back and forth, between the two wings. You can see the movement on the board here."

A master station board showed the layout of the entire research base. Motion detectors recorded all movement and even identified, via computer ID chips, who was where.

MacInnis looked at the board and saw figures moving over there, in the sealed-off spokes, moving like ants, back and forth, communicating, planning.

He licked his lips.

"We've got guns," MacInnis said.

Someone laughed. "A lot of good they'll do," the sub engineer said. "We've seen the destroyed sub, MacInnis. Remember. We've *seen* the bodies."

Again, the noise of the crowd swelled. And MacInnis started yelling, begging them to quiet down. If there was panic down here, he thought, the *seaQuest* would never come.

"Please, please," he begged, but the crowd was breaking up into smaller groups, of three and four, angry, yelling.

MacInnis couldn't do a thing to quiet them.

Then someone at the communications desk shouted.

"Hey, wait a minute. *Wait.* I'm getting contact from *seaQuest.*"

Instantly, the crowd became quiet.

MacInnis nodded. He looked down, suddenly aware that his hand was on a revolver. He didn't admit to the others that he'd never fired a gun.

The communications operator turned to MacInnis.

"They want to speak with someone, Mr. MacInnis. And they want visuals."

MacInnis shook his head. "Tell them no visuals. Tell them . . . that there's some problem down here. But tell them I can speak to them."

Morton Dell came close. "Best talk from one of the lab rooms, MacInnis. Just in case the crowd gets . . . rowdy."

MacInnis nodded. "Tell them I'll speak to the Captain . . . in a minute."

The crowd was quiet as MacInnis got down and made his way through it. They were subdued now because, MacInnis knew, they all realized that this was their only shot to get out of there.

He hurried to one of the labs.

"Let me see it," Harpe said in the darkness.

The giant screen in front of him came to life, with a freeze-framed high-definition image of Admiral William Noyce.

A voice said, "First, we have a sample of original material, Mr. Harpe."

"Okay."

And the image came to life, Noyce ordering—*ordering!*—Harpe to cease private communications with the Azores station.

It was unpleasant to listen to. Then the image froze again.

"Okay, now what?"

"Now, sir, you'll hear the text as you wrote it."

The image started moving again.

"Captain Bridger, Admiral Noyce here. The UEO board wants you to send a team into the station immediately."

Harpe searched the recreated image for any evidence of flickering, any juggling, any clue that Noyce's image had been digitized, that the words were being constructed from a memory bank of Noyce's sibilants and consonants, blends and vowels.

Harpe grinned. *I can make the old man say anything I want to,* he thought.

Like . . . *Look at me, boys and girls, I'm a circus clown.*

It was an amazing display. Where was the line between reality and illusion?

Well, that line didn't exist anymore.

The digitized Noyce continued. "Secure the main labs and specimens, Captain Bridger, and await further instructions . . ."

Again, the image came to a freeze.

"Anything else, sir?" the voice over the speakers asked.

"No . . . no. It was . . . wonderful."

And now, Harpe thought, *all we do is wait.*

CHAPTER 18

Bridger walked into the conference room, stood at the door, and smiled at Terry McShane and Richard Ernst.

"Thanks for coming to meet with me."

"Captain, I don't understand. We're almost at the station . . . I should be getting prepared." Ernst wore a cornered look. *It suits him,* Bridger thought.

Then he glanced at Terry, who looked much cooler, unflappable.

"I know, Dr. Ernst. But I'm afraid something has come up, something that requires that I ask you a few questions."

Ernst shook his head disgustedly.

"And I'm here—?" Terry said.

"Oh, I have a few questions for you too, Terry. Thought I might as well make it a little party."

"Captain, I don't find this very amusing. If you will—"

"Dr. Ernst, tell me why you're really going to the Azores station."

Ernst took a breath. "Because I'm a paleobiologist, and I'm planning on advising them about—"

Bridger shook his head. "I don't think so. I don't think

that there would be such tremendous urgency to get you to the station unless something was wrong."

Ernst shifted in his seat.

Bridger saw Terry's eyes on him. He was checking her for a flicker of understanding. Perhaps they're together, thought Bridger. And maybe he was the only one who didn't know what was going on.

"Tell me about the worms, these *Riftia pogonophosa Azores*."

Ernst raised his eyebrows, surprised that Bridger knew the name of the worms. Ernst waved the subject away with his hands. "They are giant tube worms, much like the worms found at the other vent sites—"

Bridger circled the table, coming around behind Ernst.

"No. I don't think so. You see, the other tube worms can't feed on just about anything."

"Captain, I'm afraid that the information about them is classified—"

"No, nothing is classified about this anymore. The UEO sent us everything it has on the subject. But I still don't know what *you* are supposed to do . . . and whether it's too late."

Ernst looked up. "Too late, Captain? What do you mean, too late?"

Then Bridger was at the other end of the long conference table, facing Terry. He raised a hand to Ernst, making him hold his question.

"Which brings us to you, Terry. Isn't it kind of strange that when we have to pick up Dr. Ernst, we are given orders to take *you* along . . . for a 'routine inspection' of the *seaQuest* crew in action."

Terry nodded, solemn. "Those are my orders."

Bridger nodded. "Bull. I'm sure you have orders, but I doubt they have anything to do with how the scientific and naval groups on *seaQuest* interact."

"Captain Bridger—I must insist on getting ready."

Bridger turned back to the scientist.

"What are we going to find, Dr. Ernst? Let's assume you were vacationing at SousMer. What happened at the Azores station to end that vacation? And what's happening now?"

Ernst shifted in his seat. Bridger thought that the man wouldn't say anything, a loyal Harpe employee.

But then he cleared his throat—and began talking.

MacInnis stood with the group, all of them holding their guns.

"Has there been confirmation from the *seaQuest*?" he asked the station's communications officer.

"No, Mr. MacInnis. They've only acknowledged our transmission." The communications officer turned to him. "It's like they're waiting for something."

Morton Dell cleared his throat. "Maybe they smell a rat, MacInnis."

"T-tell them that we're ready to send entry procedures. Tell them that we'll send them instructions on using the south sub bay."

"Won't they wonder," Dell said, "why we're not having them come in the main submersible entrance? It will make them a tad curious . . ."

"Something's wrong," Rodriguez said. "That's why they're not responding. God, they're not going to come in."

"No . . . no, we'll tell them that we're experiencing difficulties with one of the entrance hatches."

"Good one," Dell said sarcastically.

MacInnis looked at the board showing the location of everyone at the station, showing the two wings sealed off.

He thought of the main sub bay . . . and what it had been like when they brought the sub in, the two-man research submersible that had been dubbed *Lil' Bugger*.

How strange everything seemed . . . and how it all happened so fast . . .

So fast . . .

The submersible had been working the northern vent area, a place that was surrounded by smokers, encircled by chimneys gushing superheated toxins—H_2SO over 380 degrees hot.

Rodriguez had been monitoring the dive team—Marty Abbado and Jennifer Stern. They were experts on the chemosynthesis of the vent creatures, oceanographic micro-biologists with the highest possible reputation.

Abbado and Stern had raised some questions about the new species of worm that had been found in burrows at the center of the vent field.

At first, only dead specimens of the worm had been brought onto the station . . . It was always tricky accommodating the demands of creatures used to high pressure and the intense heat of the vent area.

And the dead creatures presented so many strange anomalies—the biggest anomaly being who was calling the shots. The bacterial colony appeared incredibly primitive, similar to communities of stromatolites that had formed over 3 billion years ago.

But this bacterial colony, this parasite, was more advanced, with different areas of the colony creature adapted for completely different purposes, each exerting control over a different part of the worm.

That's what had been learned from the dead samples.

The rest of the station was being built, with its primary focus on using the thermal energy and the unique mineral and ore resources of the area. And while that went on, plans were made for a live dissection.

A dissection that was watched by the UEO, and Harpe, *live*.

No one would forget what they saw.

Because that's when the nightmare began . . .

Lieutenant Bachmann interrupted Bridger.

"Captain, we got another message from the station. They're sounding mighty anxious, Captain. They're trying to give us information on how to enter the station." There was a pause. "Sir, they don't want us to use the main sub bay. Some problem with a door."

"I bet," Bridger said.

Ernst stood up. "Captain, I—"

There was a knock on the conference room door. Bridger said, "Come in," and Lucas ran in, breathless.

"What's the matter, Lucas? Seen a ghost?"

Lucas didn't smile. "I have something you'd better see, Captain." Lucas looked around the room. "Maybe everyone here better see."

"What is it?"

"There was a dissection performed on one of these worms, Captain. It was in the UEO file that Admiral Noyce released. I downloaded the digital video. All I'm saying is, Captain Bridger, *this* you've got to see . . ."

Bridger looked over to Ernst. "Doctor . . . if you wouldn't mind? A few more minutes . . . and, Terry, maybe you'll have something to say after you see this . . ."

"Captain," Lucas said, "I've set it up so we can watch it on the conference room screen."

Bridger took a seat and brought out his VR-PAL.

"Mr. Bachmann, tell the good folks at the station that they'll have to wait. We have a video to watch . . ."

Bridger nodded to Lucas. "Roll it, Wolenczak. The suspense is killing me."

The tape started.

Dr. Marie Thibaud, the station's chief oceanographic zoologist, had dissected the worm while Abbado and Stern looked on.

The technique she used was tricky. The live rift worm was inside a small pressurized tank of water heated to over two hundred degrees, a figure generally agreed to keep it happy.

Manipulator arms, similar to those used on the subs, were employed to make rough incisions in the worm. The idea was to see the colony creature, the parasite functioning in the worm.

The entire operation was uplinked, a live feed going to the UEO and Harpe WorldWide.

Marie talked through the delicate procedure.

"I will cut a lateral incision of one hundred centimeters from just below the mouthlike opening, and down."

Was it a mouth at the top of the creature? Watching, MacInnis didn't have a clue. It was hard to tell . . . it *looked* like a mouth, ringed with nasty teeth, or maybe it was only

169

a serrated opening of some kind. No one knew what to expect.

Certainly not what happened.

The first cut into the worm filled the tank with a murky red liquid, a thick substance. Someone said, "It has blood."

But Marie shook her head. "No, not blood. It's too thick."

Abbado said, "I'd love a sample of that."

Marie nodded. There were vials in the tank. Samples of tissue and blood could be gathered for later examination under an electron microscope.

But now, with the tank filled with a murky red liquid, it was hard, nearly impossible, to see.

Marie looked around. And she said, "We'd best wait . . . until the tank clears a bit."

A small filtering system would cleanse the water. It would take a few minutes, that's all . . . but no one knew that they didn't even have that short amount of time.

"You've seen this, I take it?" Bridger said to Ernst.

The scientist nodded. And from the sick expression on the man's face, Bridger guessed that Ernst knew what was coming up.

"I haven't seen past this point, Captain," Lucas said.

Then Bridger glanced at Terry. And from her open-mouthed expression, he was sure that she hadn't seen the tape. *Good,* he thought. *It's nice to know that we're in the dark . . . together.* And he felt a bit guilty about being so hard on her.

On the tape, he heard the chatter of the people at the dissection. Someone made a joke—"Wanna see *my* worm?" A few people laughed, someone groaned. The water was clearing . . .

Just as Bridger began to feel that something bad was about to happen . . .

Marie turned back to the tank, the water only slightly tinged red, but still the tube worm, the *Riftia Azores*, was a shadowy creature.

"Okay," Marie said. "I'll wait another minute. Then I'll—what?"

Everyone was looking at the tank, at the manipulator arms poised above the creature, one holding a sharp scapel-like device, the other grasping claws.

"That's *strange.*"

MacInnis remembered saying, "What is it?" *What's strange?* Because he didn't see anything weird. Just the worm, and some dark, blackish material underneath the now open fold of skin.

It didn't look extraordinary to him.

"God—" Marie said. "I don't know. What's going on . . . in the . . ."

Jennifer Stern leaned close, putting her face right up to the tank. MacInnis was going to tell her, *We can't see, Dr. Stern. Please, could you please—*

Marie Thibaud brought the grasping arm close to the worm, grabbed a flap of cut-open skin—

And, as she started exposing what lay beneath, the opening seemed to rupture, and something *flew* out of the open hole.

Whatever it was crashed against the glass of the tank, and Jennifer Stern screamed, reeling backward.

Whatever had been inside the worm had jumped out.

Living on its own.

Jennifer laughed, everyone laughed. It was so scary, so funny being startled like that, as if they were all kids at some spook show.

But then MacInnis, laughing too, feeling nervous, heard a sound.

Someone said, "Look at it. *Look* at what it's doing . . ."

MacInnis looked back to the tank. The thing that had been inside the worm was now smashing against the glass, pulling back, and then throwing its weight against the glass, trying to get out.

"We'd better—" MacInnis started to say.

But then he heard a *crack . . .*

171

CHAPTER 19

"Do you believe this stuff?" Lucas said.

Bridger's eyes were locked on the incredible scene. He watched the video image swirl about the room as the station's camera operator suddenly became more concerned with backing the hell away.

But someone yelled, "Tape this. Get this on tape!"

From a distance, the camera steadied and zeroed in on the tank.

The woman doing the dissection grabbed the parasite from the worm with the manipulator arm, holding it.

"Unbelievable," Terry said. "I don't—"

But the thing inside the worm split into two; a free piece of it again smacked against the glass, and Bridger heard the crack.

"Whoa!" Lucas said. "This is way too cool."

I have to talk to that boy, Bridger thought. *He evaluates all of life's experiences as though they're a big-budget special effects scene.*

"It's getting out," Terry said.

Bridger looked over at Ernst. The scientist didn't say a thing—but he was riveted by what he watched on the screen.

"This is something else," Bridger said, "eh, Dr. Ernst?"

Another smack, and the glass cracked. How strong was the thing?

And why did it want out so badly?

What Bridger saw next was the most incredible thing he'd ever seen . . .

Bar none.

It got out.

And MacInnis supposed he should have given an order of some kind. But they were in the lab, and this was completely unexpected.

Some people ran, because the thing that fell to the floor, the parasite, the piece from inside the worm, was alive, moving on the floor . . .

The pressure should have killed it; the host worm certainly looked dead, but the thing inside it was alive.

It's just a colony creature, MacInnis told himself. It can't think; it can't even live independently.

Yet it moved like a fast slug—

It moved toward one of the biotechnicians. The man screamed and stood there as if he couldn't move.

The thing was only a foot away when Rodriguez was there, holding a fire extinguisher. He shot it at the creature, and under the icy cloud of CO_2, the thing stopped moving.

Then MacInnis spoke. "Get it the hell out of here. The whole thing. Get it off the station . . ."

The cold froze it, stopped it from moving.

Just like that movie, he thought. *The Blob* . . . Didn't they freeze that and dump it in the Arctic?

Was the parasite dead?

MacInnis didn't know. He only knew that he wanted it off the station *prontissimo*.

That should have been enough warning. But everyone thought they knew what they were dealing with . . .

"Any comments, Dr. Ernst?"

The tape ended, and the scientist spun around in his chair.

174

"You saw the tape," he said flatly. "You know as much as I do."

Bridger laughed. "No—not as much as you do, Dr. Ernst. I'm not an expert in the field of—what is it?—paleobiology. I can only tell you that I've never seen anything like that before."

Now Ernst laughed. "And neither has anyone else, Captain Bridger. Unless you count what they found in Antarctica."

Finally the man seemed interested in talking.

"Antarctica?"

"About ten years ago. A giant fossil. First, it was thought to be an early predecessor of the tube worms. I mean, you must realize that until the hydrothermal vents had been discovered in the eighties, no one even knew such bizarre creatures existed."

"And what did they find in Antarctica?"

"A giant worm, immense, like the trunk of a redwood. Something tremendous. It was fossilized, stone . . . but inside was the blueprint for a creature that can only be described as 'alien.' Our best guess was that this worm was easily one billion years old. But inside were the telltale signs of other creatures, trilobites, prehistoric arthropods of all kinds. Their body chemistry complete, *absorbed* into the worm."

Ernst took a breath.

"The creature was the ultimate parasite . . . We could only be happy that it was extinct."

"And it's the same worm?" Lucas said.

Ernst shook his head. "Not exactly, but so close that it was vital that I see it."

"What do you know about the sub accident?" Bridger said.

Ernst smiled. "About as much as you do, I'm afraid. Something happened down there to one of the subs. I assume we'll find out when we go inside the station."

"We're not going in," Bridger said.

"What?"

175

"We're not entering the station." Bridger stood up. "I'm going to the bridge now to contact the UEO and tell them what I think is going on down there. I'm sure we'll be ordered to quarantine the station."

"But we have to—"

Bridger turned away from Ernst and spoke to Lucas. "Good work, Lucas. Let me know if you find anything else."

Bridger started for the door.

"Nathan—Captain, can I walk with you?"

He turned to see Terry McShane, looking rattled by the afternoon movie. "Sure."

They walked out together.

That should have ended it, MacInnis thought.

This new worm, the parasite, was dangerous, and they should have stayed the hell away.

But both Marty Abbado and Jennifer Stern had argued with MacInnis for a sub trip to the burrows of the worms, to see them up close.

"We're not going to be yanking them out," Abbado said. "What could happen?"

At the time it seemed like a good idea to MacInnis. Everyone would want to know more, the UEO, Harpe . . . and this was a *safe* way to do it.

So he let them take *Li'l Bugger* out to the vent field. MacInnis watched their progress on the VR screen, listened to them chatter while they went over to the cliff, home to the worms, the hundreds of burrows in the cliff wall . . .

They were only going to observe.

It was Marie Thibaud who first seemed apprehensive.

As *Li'l Bugger* navigated the field of smokers, snaking its way past the plumes of poisonous gasses and superheated water, Marie and MacInnis watched the screen.

The sub's camera picked up the giant clusters of albino clams and overgrown mussels, more the size of pumpkins than mussels, and then weirdly shaped crabs scuttling amid them all, looking for food.

They saw another creature there too, a giant isopod, looking like a sow bug, only of immense proportions, over three feet long—an armored tank in the vent field as it crawled on the volcanic sand.

The sub turned into the section of the vent that led to the cliffs.

"They shouldn't go there," Marie Thibaud said.

"They're only observing," Morton Dell said.

"No reason to get alarmed," Abbado answered from the sub. "We're not bringing any samples back to the station."

As they reached the field, MacInnis grew more anxious, wondering whether this was a good idea.

The sub stopped. He heard Marty and Jennifer talking, discussing how the worms seemed to slip in and out of their burrows, as if they were merely overgrown barnacles, acting like filter feeders.

"They look harmless," Abbado said.

It was the last word from the sub.

"I thought you might be upset at the third degree I was giving you," Bridger said to Terry. "I didn't mean to come down so hard—"

But Terry grabbed his arm, stopping him. "No. It's me who owes you an apology."

"What?"

"I'm not here to study the *seaQuest*'s crew . . . and how they interact."

Bridger waited.

"Ernst is Harpe's man. In fact, half the station scientists work for Geoffrey Harpe in one way or another. And the UEO and Admiral Noyce had their suspicions about what Harpe would do with this 'discovery' . . ."

"But you said you hadn't seen the tape before."

"That's true. But I was told that the discovery had implications . . ."

"Implications?"

"Whatever was inside the worm, if harnessed, could become an incredible biological weapon. Imagine what it could do if it was put in a water supply."

"Who'd be crazy enough to use it?"

"Someone who could *control* it. Enter Dr. Richard Ernst."

"If it could be controlled."

Terry nodded. "That's why Noyce wanted me on board, to watch Ernst. And Admiral Noyce told me—"

"That if *I* knew Harpe was involved in the station, I wouldn't go."

Terry nodded.

Bridger smiled. "Then, we're finally on a level playing field now. I know what's happening, I know who you are, and—I hope—I know what's waiting down at the station."

There was a pause. Terry's hand was still on his arm.

The passageway was empty; the only sound was the gentle hum of the ship.

Bridger looked at her, and the years seemed to fade away, as if it were yesterday.

"I'd better—" he started to say.

Terry leaned close and kissed him, a long, full kiss, pressing against his lips. And when they stopped, he took her hand and smiled.

"Maybe, when this is all over, you'll come to San Francisco with the ship."

"I'd love it," she said.

"Still no response from the *seaQuest*, Mr. MacInnis."

What was the problem? MacInnis wondered. They should be preparing to come down, to get everyone off. What was going on?

He bet they were wondering why they weren't using the main sub bay. *I should have made up a better story,* MacInnis thought. But he couldn't tell them that they couldn't use it because it was in one of the closed wings.

Closed . . . because . . .

The others were in there.

The ones who saw the *Li'l Bugger* when it was brought back, the manipulator arms twisted, the thick Plexiglas windows smashed open, and the crushed bodies of Marty Abbado and Jennifer Stern ripped open as if something had gone digging inside them.

They were dead. The sub smashed. It had been recovered where it had drifted away from the burrows . . .

That's what they all thought.

We were so stupid. So—

"Mr. MacInnis, something's wrong!"

MacInnis looked up to the board.

In one of those sealed wings there was a blink, a light, moving out, past one of the doors.

"That's impossible," MacInnis said.

Someone in one of those wings had gotten out, and had entered one of the other ends of the spokes, near the engineering lab.

"Looks like *nothing's* impossible anymore, Mac," Morton Dell said.

They stood there—watching as first one, then two, then more lights crossed into another section of the station.

"Seal that section," MacInnis said, screaming, hearing how he was losing it. His hand rested on the gun. Then he whispered . . .

"Contact *seaQuest* again . . ."

CHAPTER 20

CHAPTER 20

"WSKRS deployed around the station, Captain."

Bridger walked past Ortiz.

"Good, Mr. Ortiz, and let me know what they pick up. Mr. Bachmann—?"

The *seaQuest*'s communications officer turned to him. "Sir?"

"Contact the UEO and tell them I want to talk to Admiral Noyce."

As Bridger reached his command chair, Ford came over to him. "Captain, we have visuals of the vent area on screens two and three. Also, there's been another message from the station, Captain—"

Bridger nodded. "Let them wait."

Ford stood there a moment, not moving, until Bridger looked up and noticed. Obviously, something was on his exec's mind. "Captain, we're not going down?"

"Not until we know more, Mr. Ford."

"But what if they're in trouble, Captain? The people down there might need help."

Right . . . and Bridger wondered whether Ford thought that maybe there was a crisis of nerves here. Bridger looked up to the screens, at the vent fields, a dark, smoky area except for the murky lights of the station sitting to one edge of the field.

"We're going to have to wait on that," Bridger said.

Ford nodded. "Aye, aye, sir . . ."

Bachmann said, "Captain, I have UEO headquarters. They're putting you directly through to Admiral Noyce."

"Good."

Captain Bridger waited.

MacInnis watched the lights on the board—each light a person—as they entered the research wing.

"How the hell are they getting in!" MacInnis said. "What's going on there!" The station crew behind him were mumbling, scared. Then a man yelled.

"Someone has to stop them!"

MacInnis licked his lips. He felt the panic growing in the room. They were trapped down here—God—and things are unraveling . . .

The third section—the research pod and the arm leading to it—was now sealed. But if they got through one wing, then maybe they could break through another.

Morton Dell came up beside him. "Any volunteers for that job, MacInnis?"

"I-I think we should all stay here."

Dell looked up at the board. "And wait for them to come?"

Rodriguez came over. "Dell's right—"

"Why, thank you, Julio. I thought you despised me—"

"Shut up," Rodriguez said. The engineer turned back to MacInnis. "We can't sit here and wait for them to come."

"Any word from *seaQuest*?" MacInnis yelled to Booker, the communications officer.

Booker shook his head and MacInnis licked his lips . . . "Right. Okay, Dell, you go down to the entrance and make sure no one gets through."

Dell laughed. "You must think I'm crazy. No, Mr. MacInnis, I'm only waiting to get out of this hellhole with my skin intact."

MacInnis turned to Rodriguez. "Julio—"

"Hey, that's a crazy idea. I don't—"

MacInnis lowered his voice. "All you have to do is stay by the passage and make sure no one gets through. That's all. The passageway doors are electrically locked. They *can't* get through. Just stay there with your gun."

Rodriguez shook his head, obviously upset. But, MacInnis thought, he recognized that what I'm saying makes sense.

Rodriguez nodded. "Okay, but, damn it, let me know when the sub comes."

"Okay." And Rodriguez turned toward the recently infiltrated section . . . while MacInnis hurried to the communications console.

Captain Gerry Wilson's smiling face was on the screen.

"Let me speak to Admiral Noyce," Bridger said.

Bridger guessed that the tone of his voice didn't leave any room for bureaucratic runaround.

"One moment, Captain Bridger," Wilson said.

Noyce appeared.

"Admiral—"

"Captain."

He knows what's coming, Bridger thought. He felt bad that Noyce, a good friend, couldn't be trusted, that there would always be this wall between them.

Bridger started to tell Noyce why the *seaQuest* shouldn't go down to the station . . . while Noyce listened.

Geoffrey Harpe called out in the darkness.

"Is it ready?"

"Yes, Mr. Harpe," the disembodied voice answered.

Harpe watched the dialogue between Noyce and Bridger. He looked at Bridger, thinking, *It seems like a century ago that we were friends, back when that word actually had some meaning for me.*

Back when Bridger liked heavy metal music and practical jokes.

Now, all their jokes were over.

183

Bridger was explaining why *seaQuest* shouldn't go down to the station.

"All set," Harpe called out.

Noyce was about to answer Bridger.

"And . . . now!" Harpe said.

Noyce nodded, listening to Nathan. He was right, of course. The risks were too great. There were a lot of lives at stake, and a discovery like this could have tremendous implications. The UEO's science people wanted to see these new vent creatures.

But it was way too risky.

Noyce cleared his throat. "Nathan—"

The image of the *seaQuest*'s captain disappeared from the screen.

"What?"

"Captain," Noyce spoke in measured tones, serious, his voice steady. "We've looked at all the information. The station appears secure, and the UEO board has authorized entry into the station—with the highest priority."

That is *strange,* Bridger thought.

Just a minute ago, he had been convinced that Noyce was about to agree with him that it was way too risky to enter the station. Now the Admiral was telling him, *ordering* him, to go down.

Bridger shifted in his seat.

"Admiral, I don't think that you understand. We've seen the dissection of this thing they found down there. Something has happened; there's been some kind of incident."

Every now and then, Noyce seemed to look away as if distracted.

"We have no evidence of that. Your mission is to deliver an expert to the station, Captain Bridger. Someone who'd know the real danger—*If* there was any danger, Dr. Ernst would be the one to tell us. It's not a decision that you are empowered to make."

Bridger stood up. "Not empowered? Admiral, this is my command. And you are asking me to send men into a

184

situation where I don't know what the hell is happening—"

Commander Ford came close to Bridger. "Captain—" he said, and Bridger looked over at Ford, seeing that his exec was cautioning him. Bridger shook his head. "You don't know what's going on down there, Bill. How can you—"

Noyce turned away again, and Bridger wished he knew what was wrong here, what kept distracting Noyce, pulling him away.

"That is precisely the reason you *have* to go there. We *don't* know what's happening. And Dr. Ernst will apprise us of the dangers . . ."

Even the language use seemed strained.

"So now I take orders from Dr. Ernst?"

There was a pause. "You have only one order, Captain Bridger. Get into that station, escort Dr. Ernst. And I expect you to carry out that order immediately."

Bridger stared at the screen. Noyce blinked. He looked distracted, as if something were wrong—

"Yes, Admiral," Bridger said. Bridger hit a switch on his left control panel.

The link to the UEO went down . . . and Bridger sat perfectly still.

Noyce pressed a button on his desk console.

"Captain Wilson, what's the problem here? What happened to *seaQuest*?"

Noyce heard Wilson's voice . . .

"I don't know, Admiral. There was no problem with the two-way link, the Net is still open to us. We just weren't getting *seaQuest*'s signal . . . and they weren't getting ours."

"Well, fix it," Noyce said, imagining the *seaQuest,* cruising closer to the vent field.

Harpe watched the replay. The digitized image of Noyce was nearly perfect, the way he spoke, the way his face moved.

Nearly real.

Almost.

Harpe froze a frame. "There's a bit of a flutter there. Why is that?"

Again, the voice of the computer technician . . . "Facial gestures, eye movement, lips, et cetera, are all linked to speech, Mr. Harpe. And while we have a large library of Noyce's sounds, there are still minute gaps, times when the program doesn't know what to do with the digitized image. Only a millisecond or so, but it's a blip."

Harpe nodded. Yes, it was there, but all but unnoticeable. It could easily be explained as a problem in the link, or even a transmission delay. It was nothing to worry about . . .

"Monitor the *seaQuest*'s communications," Harpe said. "In case they try to contact the UEO again."

Which, judging from the look on Bridger's face, appeared unlikely.

Now all Harpe had to do was wait.

"Mr. Ford, plot coordinates to take us close to the station."

"We're going in, sir?"

"No, Mr. Ford, not *we* . . . I'm going in. Mr. Bachmann, contact the Azores station. If they've got visuals, put them on the screen. And tell them to prepare for our arrival."

"Sir, they've already uploaded the boarding procedure to be used. There's a sub bay at the southern end of the station. It's not the main bay . . ."

"Right," Bridger said. "That's because there's probably something wrong with the main bay. And we won't know what that is, boys and girls, until we get there. Mr. Ortiz, where's that WSKRS scan of the station you promised me?"

Ortiz spun around on his chair. "Anytime you want it, Captain, I can put it on the monitors."

Bridger walked directly under one of the VR screens, one showing the Azores station sitting in an open area at the edge of the vent field. The exterior lights of the research facility faintly illuminated the nearest smokers, the slender rock chimneys gushing forth poisonous black smoke.

Bridger saw some red shrimp swarming near the station. A few angler fish huddled by the sandy floor, idly watched by some lantern fish.

"Mr. Ortiz, keep this screen on live feed, and use the other two for the WSKRS data."

The two screens on either side of the center monitor suddenly came to life, and Bridger watched a series of graphical displays swirl by.

Ortiz was sifting through the information for something of interest.

"Nathan—" Bridger heard a voice behind him, and he spun around to see Kristin Westphalen standing there.

"Yes, Kristin—what's up?"

"You're going into the station?"

Bridger nodded.

"Don't you think that's a bit risky, Nathan? We don't know what's going on in there."

Bridger pointed a finger at the scientist. "You're exactly right there. We *don't* know what's going on in there. But an order is an order."

Westphalen cleared her throat. "Then I want to come—"

"Out of the question."

"But this is an opportunity to see what they've been working on. These creatures are . . . incredible."

"We'll bring you back one. A dead one."

"Nathan, please. I'm the ship's science chief. I deserve—"

"Captain, I have a schematic of the station showing the point of entry," Ortiz said.

"Approach course plotted, sir," Ford said.

There was no time for a lengthy debate with Dr. Westphalen.

"Bring our cruising speed down ten knots, Mr. Ford."

Westphalen touched Bridger's arm. "Captain, I must insist—"

But Bridger turned back to her, shrugging off her arm. "No. You don't understand, Kristin. I don't want to go down there. I don't even think I *should* go down there. But I've been ordered to take Ernst there. But that doesn't mean that I will risk anyone else on the *seaQuest*. Is that clear enough?"

Bridger turned away from Westphalen.

He'd been rough on her, but he didn't want this argument to go on. And Bridger needed to make sure everyone else heard it . . . including Ford.

"Captain, do you want to alert the submersible unit in the moon pool?"

Bridger nodded. "Good idea. Prepare the sea shuttle. I'm going down there—"

"Captain," Ford said, "I should go, sir. It's—"

Bridger kept walking away. "Have you been listening? Not a chance, Mr. Ford." He called back to his exec. "This is my baby. Just make sure Dr. Ernst is ready. And give me a good pilot for the shuttle."

"Lieutenant Maklin is available."

"Good. And Mr. Ford, there is one thing—you can monitor us all the way. Believe it or not, I *do* want to come back."

CHAPTER 21

"They're coming!"

Booker, the communications officer, yelled out the news and everyone cheered. But MacInnis only smiled faintly, and he kept his eyes on the third, now exposed, arm of the station.

He saw the blip representing Rodriguez, standing guard.

"He's got balls, that one," Dell said.

"Not like some of us," MacInnis said.

"Oh, you're not holding it against me because I wouldn't play guard for you? I've seen what those things can do, MacInnis. I'm not stupid."

"No—just gutless."

"Ouch. I didn't see *you* volunteering to go there."

"I have to meet the *seaQuest* . . . I have to talk to them."

"I'm sure we could have found someone to pinch-hit for you."

MacInnis saw Dell look up at the tracking board. There was Rodriguez, on one side of the locked doors, and there were these other blips, gathered antlike against the electronically locked doors.

"They sure look as if they want to get out," Dell said.

"Are you sure they're all contaminated . . . Are you sure that there aren't some people wanting to escape?"

"I'm sure."

"*seaQuest* has downloaded the station schema, Mr. MacInnis," Booker called out. "But there's something else."

"What—what is it?"

"We're being watched. Something's outside gathering data, scanning the station. A couple of things . . . probes of some kind." Booker looked over with a sick look on his face. "They're checking us out, Mr. MacInnis."

"Uh-oh, Mac," Dell said. "Hope they don't see that we have a *petite* problem. Wouldn't want to scare them away."

Come on, MacInnis thought. Just keep coming.

Ortiz looked at the information picked up by Junior.

Power was off in two—no, three wings of the station. Completely shut down, all power off.

Now what could be the reason for that? Whatever the reason, that was probably why they couldn't use the main sub bay. Still, it was something to tell Captain Bridger.

So Ortiz called down to the moon pool.

"There," Dr. Shimura said, fitting the communication chip into Darwin's head. "Now, how does that feel?"

The dolphin still didn't look right, his eyes wild, upset.

"Don't worry. I'll have you hooked up in a minute, and we'll find out how you're feeling, eh?"

The dolphin slapped his tail fin against the surface of the water, sending a spray up to the low ceiling of the medical center.

"Trying to water some of my bromeliads? I'm afraid they don't like saltwater, my friend."

Shimura glanced up at the screen in the corner of the lab, showing the Azores research station—their destination— and the alien terrain of the hydrothermal vent field.

"No, Darwin," Shimura said, tightening the communication harness, "I don't want to go there either . . ."

▲   ▲   ▲

Bridger opened the door to the moon pool, and walked right into Terry McShane. He saw Ernst standing by one of the bays as the sea shuttle cruised into place.

"What do you think you're doing down here?" he asked.

"I'm going."

Bridger laughed. "I don't think so."

But Terry didn't smile. "Captain—" She lowered her voice. "My responsibility is to watch Ernst. That's what I'm here for—"

"No, no—that doesn't include taking you into a potentially dangerous situation."

He saw Ernst look over.

"I'll watch him for you." Bridger saw Lieutenant Tim Maklin come out of the shuttle. The sea shuttle was an awkwardly shaped submersible, looking more like a light fixture than a ship. Though it could be operated by a single pilot, it held up to thirty personnel and nearly two tons of cargo.

"You're staying, and that's it—"

"I can have Admiral Noyce tell you—"

Bridger stopped and turned. "Tell me what? Give me another damn order? You know, I knew it was a mistake to leave my island, to think that this was an opportunity to do something—"

Terry reached out for him, grabbed his hand, and squeezed it.

"It *is* an opportunity, Nathan. You're right. What's down there could be dangerous. And there's no one better to be going in than you. But no one's stopping you from doing your job. Please—" She squeezed his hand again. "Don't stop me from doing mine."

Maklin was helping Ernst into the shuttle.

"Nathan—you'll have to check the station. Let *me* watch Ernst."

"Captain—"

It was Ford's voice over the moon pool's speaker. "Captain, we're ready for shuttle launch here. We're one klick away from Azores Station."

"Nathan—it's not a favor . . . it's my job."

Bridger ran his fingers through his hair. "I've got to be crazy . . . Come on—"

He led her over to the waiting shuttle, bobbing like a bizarre children's toy.

Well, thought Dr. Westphalen, *if I can't go one way . . . I'll go* another.

She reached down and slipped a VR-goggle unit on her head. Normally, she hated the things. They were so clumsy, and she rarely felt the need to be totally immersed in the virtual images.

But Nathan had left her no choice.

She hit a key on her console, and, inside the goggles, she was suddenly surrounded by a misty gray fog.

"Of course," she said . . . *Of course there would be nothing to see.*

She hadn't released the VR probe yet.

She slipped her hands into the data gloves. She wasn't expert at using them, but she had seen Lieutenant Krieg move the VR probe effortlessly through the most delicate maneuvers.

Still, she'd have to do this herself.

The VR probe sat in a compartment that could be opened to the sea.

Westphalen pulled back on her right index finger, curling it. And the gray scene in front of her changed . . . as the door to the outside opened.

The water near the exterior of the ship was lit by the faint glow of *seaQuest*'s running lights. But Westphalen curled another finger, and the probe's bright tungsten lamp came on.

Now she could see a good twenty meters ahead . . . mostly the organic "snow" that constantly fell, bits of plant and animal material sinking to the bottom.

The scientist waited patiently for the sea shuttle to begin its trip.

CHAPTER 22

The entrance hatch to the sea shuttle closed—and automatically locked. A green light came on on the control panel.

"Captain, we're cleared to disengage from the docking bay."

Bridger turned back to Ernst and Terry sitting behind him. "If you're strapped in, we'll be leaving. You can watch our progress on the monitor above you."

"Captain," Ernst said, "how long will this take?"

"Not long at all, Dr. Ernst. Mr. Maklin, let's get moving."

Maklin took the control stick and Bridger felt the shuttle moving. The hatch windows were already under, showing the brightly lit water of the *seaQuest*'s moon pool.

But as Maklin turned the minisub around, Bridger saw the channel that led to the sea opening, and the vent field waiting outside.

Julio Rodriguez held the electron-mag gun tightly in his hand. He stood by the sealed door and thought:

There's no way someone's coming through that door. And if they do, they'll be toast.

He had the gun set to kill. Quickly, instantly, painlessly. Not that he cared.

Rodriguez looked at the sealed bulkhead door. The only way it could be opened was if someone at the communications center released it.

Rodriguez took a step closer to it.

If the lights on the control board were to be believed, the others were just on the other side. The others, the infected ones . . .

What the hell were they doing? he wondered. *Standing there, waiting for something to happen?* As Rodriguez waited, he thought of the *seaQuest* waiting outside, and how he'd breathe so much easier once he was out of this hole, this *trap.*

A drop of sweat fell off his brow. It's not that hot, he thought.

Why am I sweating?

And then he heard a noise from behind the door.

The shuttle cleared the sea doors smoothly, and Bridger went from looking at the monitor to looking at the front port.

The research station was almost lost amid the twisting caverns and valleys that girded the vent field.

A few more lights on the station's exterior wouldn't hurt, Bridger thought. As it was now, it barely stood out in the blackness.

But the station's lights still illuminated the nearby smokers, and the shuttle's lights picked up one of the WSKRS probes hovering nearby. Inside *seaQuest,* Bridger knew, everyone was watching their progress.

"Lieutenant, can we aim a camera into the field?"

"Yes, sir."

Bridger turned back to Dr. Ernst. "Doctor, where did they find this new specimen?"

Ernst leaned forward, looking at the scene in the front port, and then the monitor. The scene on the monitor flipped, and now there was a close-up view of the murky field.

"It's hard to tell, Captain Bridger. But the seafloor in these caverns is dotted with smokers. Up to now, we've never seen anything quite like it. There's tremendous heat all through there, incredible volcanic activity. But the burrow to the new worms, the *Riftia Azores*, is through there."

Ernst pointed at a spot lost in blackness.

And Bridger guessed that he wouldn't be getting much of a look at the worm field. No, not without going closer. He glanced back at Terry. She was looking at the monitor— and she seemed nervous. Perhaps, Bridger thought, I should have insisted that she stay on the ship. The hell with the UEO, the hell with Noyce—

He smiled at her, and said, "Still glad you came?"

"Wouldn't miss it for the world."

Nathan laughed.

Westphalen released the VR probe, and it started traveling some three hundred meters behind the shuttle. Of course, Westphalen knew that the WSKRS probe would pick up the VR probe, but she banked that Ortiz would be focused on the station.

Westphalen raised the two data gloves in front of her goggle-covered head, and—out in the deep ocean—she saw the VR raise its manipulator arms. And there was this giddy feeling, a rush of excitement as she felt herself *merge* with the probe.

Then, by moving her fingers, she turned the probe to the right.

And there was the vent field . . .

As the shuttle continued toward the research station, Westphalen was engulfed by the blackness of the vent area, the dark shadows of the vent columns, and the terrible excitement of venturing into an unknown world.

MacInnis touched Marie Thibaud's shoulder.

"I-I'd like to leave you here while I meet the *seaQuest* people."

Thibaud nodded. "What if—if they refuse to take us?"

MacInnis shook his head violently. "No, there's no way

they'd do that. They have to take us. They couldn't leave us down here. It would be murder."

MacInnis looked up at the board, the lights gathered by the locked bulkhead.

"It's as if," Marie said, "they think that they'll be able to get in."

MacInnis licked his lips. "I have to go meet the shuttle. If anything happens, tell me."

She nodded, and MacInnis left.

The VR probe sailed past a smoker. A digital readout in the goggles recorded the increasing temperature . . . 200 degrees, 300 degrees . . . and still climbing.

Westphalen made the probe cut to the left, closer to one of the canyon walls. The probe was tested to 500 degrees— still it wasn't a good idea to push it to its limits.

Strangely, Westphalen felt as if she were *there,* that she was floating in the vent area. She took a breath, as if the water threatened to drown her, cutting off her air.

The probe's light was a high-powered tungsten lamp invented for deep-sea use by Canada's Can-Dive crew. It weighed nothing, but it cast a tremendously powerful beam that cut through the darkness.

She could aim the lamp by simply moving another finger, and now she checked the seafloor directly below the probe. She saw some giant sea stars, spindly echinoderms often found at vent areas.

There, crawling over one of the sea stars, she spotted an albino crab holding something ragged in a claw. A bit of fish, some squid, part of another crab—it was too hard to tell.

The crab stopped scuttling, and it looked up at the probe— at Westphalen. Its black eyes seemed to pop out of its shell as it studied her.

It raised its free claw.

"Going to grab me, are you?" Westphalen said.

She thought that she was easily high enough, but—just to be safe, she raised the probe, and—

She *bumped* into something. The rattle, and the sound of

a clunk made her feel as if she had been crawling under a table and quickly stood up.

She looked up—and the probe "looked" up.

There, scurrying away, looking more like an eel, was a vicious-appearing needle-nosed fish, a good ten feet long with a narrow mouth that ended in a nasty snout filled with teeth.

The needle-nose curled in on itself, its pride bruised, perhaps considering whether it should attack the probe.

Westphalen raised her arms.

"Better not come after me," she said, "or I'll grab you with these!"

She made the probe's claws open and shut, and the needle-nose, after a brief pause, shot away.

Westphalen turned her attention back to the view ahead.

She was nearing the center of the field. The cliff wall, the place where the strange *Riftia Azores* lived, was directly ahead.

She checked the temperature on the meter inside the goggles—320 degrees—and climbing.

Westphalen continued into the field.

"Captain, the docking area is on the left of the screen. It's actually a supply hatch, but the sea shuttle should fit fine."

Right, thought Bridger—but looking at the station, so quiet, so still, he didn't buy the idea that the main sub door was jammed.

Something's wrong down there, he guessed—*and we don't know what it is.*

"Take it slowly, Mr. Maklin. Nice and easy."

"Attention, *seaQuest* shuttle craft. We are ready for docking procedure."

Bridger saw a small sea door open at the south end of the station. The angle of entry looked awkward, maybe dangerous—

"Is that okay, Lieutenant? Can you get through there?" Bridger asked.

"Yes, sir—should be no problem if I take it slowly."

Bridger nodded, and he looked back at Ernst. The man with the secrets, Bridger thought.

And, if we're lucky, the next few minutes should tell the story.

Rodriguez leaned close to the sealed bulkhead. There was all this *noise* behind there. What the hell were they doing? he wondered.

He picked up his radio.

"MacInnis, what are they doing? I'm hearing all this—"

"MacInnis isn't here, Julio. He's gone to meet the sub."

"Marie, what's it show on the board? They're doing . . . something in there."

Rodriguez waited. *C'mon, tell me what's going on.*

He held the gun tightly, almost wishing she'd see someone, one of them walking toward him, and he could pull the trigger. *Zap!*

"There's nothing, Julio. Nothing except— Oh, God. Oh—"

Rodriguez froze. Now, wasn't this great? Wasn't this a great thing to hear?

He felt his gut go tight. The noise sounded different.

"Marie," he yelled into the radio, "what is it—what—"

And Rodriguez heard the sound *around* him . . .

410. 420 degrees . . .

Westphalen almost imagined that she could feel the heat. The probe was good to over 500. Have to remember that, she told herself there was nothing to worry about.

She passed a field of ordinary rift worms—if you could use the word "ordinary" to describe anything that towered twenty feet or more and looked like an alien forest, a nightmare dreamed up by Lovecraft.

The probe sailed right over the field of worms.

An alien life form, that's what they were, Westphalen thought. Life *not* as we know it. Something that feeds on poisons!

The chemical synthesis of food . . . Perhaps, Westphalen wondered, there had been a time when these two life forms battled for supremacy on the planet—chemosynthesizers versus photosynthesizers, and the loser took the darkest, deadliest piece of real estate on the planet.

And—

The probe passed a rocky cliff—and something changed.

Westphalen caught her breath and stopped the probe. The view was incredible. Here was an immense underwater canyon, the floor filled with smokers, rows of chimneys gushing forth poisonous sulfide hydroxide. The combined smoky cloud made a giant layer, a covering that gathered at one end of the cavern—

Hiding whatever was at the other end.

Right now Westphalen felt as if she didn't want to go down there. It wasn't real. She was safe inside the *seaQuest*.

Then why don't I feel safe?

But she made the probe inch forward, slowly forward, then down, closer to the chimneys, closer to the mouth of the cavern and the burrows hidden under the cloud.

Surprisingly, the shuttle easily navigated the station entrance. Bridger went back to Terry.

"Can you stick with me once we're inside?"

Terry looked over at Ernst, making sure that he was occupied, looking out the front screen.

"I have to watch him," Terry whispered. "But I'll be careful."

"Captain, we're ready to surface."

"Okay, Mr. Maklin. Let's enter the station."

Noyce looked at Wilson. "What's wrong? How do we simply 'lose' contact with the *seaQuest*, Captain?"

Gerry Wilson stood in front of Noyce, looking confused. "Admiral, they're checking it down in TeleCom—but everything else seems fine, except for the link to the sub. Perhaps the problem's there."

"Perhaps . . . perhaps . . . Christ, get your butt down there and tell them I want to be linked to *seaQuest* now."

Admiral Noyce was left in the dark, left to imagine what was happening.

▲   ▲   ▲

Marie Thibaud looked at the board . . . The lights were moving first one, then two—

As if they were slowly getting through the locked door.

"What's happening?" she said. The communications officer shrugged.

"I don't know, we show all the doors locked, nothing is happening—"

Morton Dell walked up to the board, looking at the lights. "Oh, I'd say that *something* is happening." He turned to Marie. "They're moving, Marie. And, unless I'm wrong, you'd better tell MacInnis that our friends from *seaQuest* will be in for a bit of a surprise."

Yes, Marie thought. MacInnis will have to be told. But first she'd have to tell Rodriguez to get out of there.

"Julio," she said. "Rodriguez, are you still there? Look, we've—"

Rodriguez instinctively backed away from the door, listening to Marie's voice.

"The board shows them moving there. They seem to be getting through—"

Rodriguez shook his head. *No, no one's getting through.* He was staring at the sealed door. *No one is moving!*

He took another step backward.

"That's impossible. I don't see anyone. Your machine's wrong. No one's getting through. There's no way—"

Then—a sick moment—he heard the sound again.

A little skittering noise . . . first to the side, then above him, and—

Now he knew where they were.

Westphalen plunged into the black cloud. She activated a guidance system on the probe that would keep it from ramming into rocks. But she'd still have to keep a close watch on the temperature gauge herself.

She had the probe do a chemical analysis of the water. And there were the usual suspects—the H_2SO and other chemical toxins—but now there was something else. There was carbon . . .

At first, the probe displayed the presence of only trace elements of carbon. Then the numbers started climbing.

Free-floating carbon was a sign that something organic had been in the water and was now dead, destroyed, burned—it was hard to tell.

The cloud turned to complete black, and the probe's powerful light illuminated nothing. And Westphalen felt as if she were swimming in the murky water.

Again, she hit something—a chunk of something that smacked into the 360-degree lens of the probe and then pushed it away.

But it was impossible to see what it was in the blackness.

Then—the cloud appeared to thin.

The probe's light carried for a few centimeters, then as the fog cleared, she could see for more than a meter or two.

The fog cleared further, and Westphalen finally saw the burrows.

The shuttle popped to the surface, and the water ran off its sleek bubble top as if it were a swimmer popping to the surface.

It didn't look as big as MacInnis had imagined. Was it big enough to get everyone off? Would they have to make two trips? Was there going to be a problem . . . ?

The radio at the service bay came to life.

"MacInnis, they're breaking out. The board shows them getting out!"

It was Marie. They were breaking out—*now*—just as the sub arrived.

"Marie—s-start bringing people down here." Yes, that was the best idea. Get people down to the shuttle now, and make the *seaQuest* people take them on.

MacInnis grabbed his gun.

And if I have to, I'll use this, he thought.

"Get them down here!" he yelled.

The hatch to the shuttle started opening, a spaceship from another world.

MacInnis waited.

Ford walked away from the communications console, back to Navigation.

He didn't like this standing around, waiting. And it wasn't only because EVAs were his job. Bridger was still new to the ship. Maybe he was out of practice, out of touch.

What kind of risk was he putting them in by doing this?

Ford looked at the monitors, wishing that there were cameras inside the station, that they had visuals running and that he could see Bridger as he made his way into the station—

Doubting the man—

"Wait a minute. What the—" Bachmann said.

Ford looked over at Bachmann. "What is it, Mr. Bachmann?"

"I'm getting a live sound feed, from inside the station—"

"So, what's the—"

"Listen—it's coming from *inside* the sealed modules of the station."

Then the voice, a new voice, filled the bridge.

And—Ford thought—the temperature dropped another twenty degrees.

CHAPTER 23

Bridger got out of the shuttle first, and he saw a man standing on the small metallic dock. The man looked as if he hadn't slept in a week.

Bridger went up to him, as Terry got off and Ernst stumbled a bit, clambering out of the sub.

"Captain, thank you for coming." The man stuck out his hand. Bridger shook the man's hand. "I'm Station Chief Ralph MacInnis. I have my people . . ."

Bridger looked around. He saw two doors leading from the sub pool.

". . . coming down here now and they're ready to get taken off the station."

"Whoa. Wait a minute. 'Taken off the station'? What are you talking about?"

MacInnis licked his lips. "You know what happened here—" His eyes were wild.

"I know you found something that the UEO is concerned about—"

MacInnis laughed, a nervous, demented sound. "No. You see—we told Harpe. I told him what happened. Harpe said he told the UEO about the accident. A sub crashed. And when we brought the people back in—"

MacInnis's eyes went back and forth, from Terry, to Bridger, to—

Ernst. And Ernst spoke.

"You brought them in here? You had the worms brought in here?"

MacInnis shook his head. "No. I mean, we didn't know they were in the sub . . . I mean—" He looked at Bridger almost apologetically. "We didn't *know* they were inside the people." He grinned. "Hiding, waiting."

Bridger looked away and whispered to Terry.

"This isn't good. I thing we'd better—"

"Your samples, you have samples of the worms in your lab?" Ernst asked.

MacInnis nodded. "We have tissue samples there, the tests on the creatures' cells. But the lab is—"

Ernst started walking down the metal ramp to one of the doors.

"I know where the lab is."

Bridger yelled at him. "Ernst, where do you—"

Ernst stopped. "Captain. We have to get those samples and get out of here."

He turned and started running.

"I've got to follow him," Terry said. "Harpe can't get his hands—"

And then the other door opened, and people, the research station crew—all with the same terrified, wide-eyed stare that MacInnis wore—came into the sub bay.

MacInnis grabbed Bridger. "You have to get us out, Captain. Now!" MacInnis pulled out the gun and pressed it against Bridger's side. "So you tell everyone they can come on board."

Ford listened to the voice.

"Repeat, this is Dr. Laurence Petersen. We need to warn you that we have been imprisoned by the others on the station . . . They have attempted to keep us locked up in two wings of the station."

Ford looked at Bachmann. Cold, colder . . . wondering . . . *What the hell's going on here?*

"The others, the ones you are meeting, have been contaminated. They have been infiltrated by an opportunistic creature. Do not approach them. Come to the station's main sub pool. There are people here who need—"

Ford ran back to the command chair.

He hit a switch.

"Captain Bridger!" he yelled.

He waited a terrible millisecond for the *seaQuest*'s captain to respond . . .

The smoky haze cleared, and—God—there they were, hundreds, maybe thousands of blackish holes, the burrows. And as the VR probe slowly, gingerly approached the burrows, Westphalen saw the worms stick their bodies out.

She saw the mouthlike opening at the end, the tiny rows of teeth.

They seem aware *that I'm here,* Westphalen thought.

Closer, and Westphalen remembered to check the recorder. A tiny red light blinked, indicating that what she was seeing was being recorded.

But this was more like being there, looking into those blackish holes, wondering how the creature established itself here.

Then she looked at the great chunk of volcanic rock, the cliff that was the moundlike home of the worms.

The probe floated closer to the burrows.

In full three-dimensional detail, the worms came out, then they slid back in, out and in, as if tasting the presence of the probe in the water, sensing it . . . feeling it.

One worm seemed to tilt at a funny angle—

And then—with Westphalen looking right at it—one worm leapt out of its burrow, its jagged-tooth mouth open, heading right toward the probe.

Rodriguez backed up. And he had this feeling that if he just went a step at a time, slowly, cautiously, it would all be *okay.*

Because then—he wouldn't be panicking. And as long as he didn't panic, everything would be . . . *fine*.

But then the sounds kept following him, surrounding him. With every step he took, there was this noise from the sides of the corridor, from above and around him, then *passing* him.

"What are they doing!" he screamed in the radio.

Marie's voice sounded so far away.

"I-I don't know. Maybe the readout is wrong. We're going down to the sub now, Julio. Come back—"

He was listening, backing up, when he heard a pop, and the clank of metal falling to the walkway.

Rodriguez held his gun tight. He turned around, slowly, again reminding himself, *I mustn't panic* . . .

He heard a grunt, and then he saw Dr. Laurence Petersen, the head of the geophysics team. And Petersen looked okay, sure—except for a bit of black grease on his cheek and a nasty cut under his neck—*he looked okay . . . nothing wrong at all!*

Petersen looked up and smiled at him.

"Oh, Julio, I didn't see you there . . ."

Petersen kept crawling out. *Mustn't panic,* Rodriguez told himself. *Must keep my cool.*

"Those shafts are so damn narrow." Petersen got to his feet. "Thought I might get stuck." The scientist grinned.

Got to shoot him, Rodriguez thought. *It's not Petersen. Got to kill the thing before—*

Petersen's smile seemed to widen, then the mouth was wide open and—

Rodriguez pulled the trigger.

Ernst ran down the corridor. The woman ran behind him, and Ernst wondered why the hell she was following him. *What does she want with me?* he thought.

He had the layout of the base memorized.

If they abandoned this base, there might never be another chance to get this material, to study this incredible life form. Or worse, he could see the UEO giving an order to destroy the whole site.

If that happened—it would be more than an extinction.

It would remove a life form that traced back to a time when the future of the planet was unclear, when life could have become something strange, alien . . .

Ernst reached a sliding door and hit the button to open it. He looked behind him and heard steps, the sound of the woman running.

He turned back to the door, opening so slowly, the door to the main lab of the Azores station . . .

Bridger didn't move.

"Tell them!" MacInnis yelled. And Bridger smelled the man's fear, the terror.

If the people from the station were to come on board the *seaQuest*—without being quarantined—they would release that terror on the surface.

"I can't do that," Bridger said. "Look—you don't know if any of your people have been infected."

MacInnis made the gun dig painfully into Bridger's side.

"They're fine—but they won't be fine if they stay in the station. The others are *loose,*" he hissed in Bridger's ear. "They're loose, and we have to leave."

Bridger saw the station crew, the technicians, the research scientists, the dive teams—fifteen, twenty people lining up as though they were about to take a Circle Line cruise around Manhattan.

Bridger looked over to the opening to the sub.

Was this all being picked up by Ford? Did Ford have any bright ideas?

"I'm going to count to three, Captain."

Bridger wondered whether MacInnis had any experience with weapons. He was the station chief, a white-collar man—obviously more loyal to Harpe than the UEO.

Bridger played a dangerous game in his head, weighing the possibilities, wondering what would happen if he should make a move, if he should try to get away from MacInnis's probing gun.

"One . . ."

Bridger thought he heard something in the hatch.

The radio at his side came to life.

"Captain, is everything okay there?"

It was Ford, and Bridger smiled at that. Gee—could things get any better?

"They can go in with or without your cooperation, Captain . . . Two . . ."

And we know what number comes next, eh, boys and girls? thought Bridger.

The people pressed close together on the metal ramp leading to the shuttle.

"Captain, what is your status down—?" Ford asked.

MacInnis opened his mouth. And then there was movement at the entrance hatch.

Bridger held his breath.

Westphalen watched the creature leap at the probe. For an instant it was caught in the glare of the high-intensity lights. She saw the creature's open mouth and watched the teeth move, back and forth, as though—

Westphalen recoiled in her chair . . .

As though there were muscles connected to the teeth, and they could move, grinding back and forth.

There was a painful exploding noise, and then there was nothing in the goggles. A dead screen.

The probe was destroyed, and Westphalen wanted to watch it all again, to see these terrible strange creatures again.

But now it was impossible.

Shimura had one eye on the monitor showing the research station while he checked the communication chip, making sure that it was in place behind Darwin's bulbous head.

"There we are," Shimura said. "Now you should—"

But Darwin kicked away. The dolphin swam back and forth crazily, and then there was a burst of static on the speaker.

Shimura thought that maybe there was something wrong with the communication device. Perhaps it had gotten damaged, though Bachmann said it was fine, that—

The static cleared, and Shimura heard Darwin's synthesized voice.

"There is danger . . ."

Shimura watched the dolphin swim back and forth, kicking at the water.

"No, Darwin, there isn't any—"

But the creature jumped out of the water.

"There is danger. There is . . . death. Outside."

Shimura shook his head. What could the dolphin know? He'd been here the whole time.

Nothing. Unless . . .

Shimura stared at the dolphin, whose eyes were wild with fright.

Unless Darwin *sensed* something. Shimura came closer to the tank.

"What is it, Darwin? What do you know?"

"There is death. It's coming to Bridger . . . It's coming *here . . .*"

Shimura rubbed the head of the dolphin, and decided that he'd better tell Commander Ford.

Ortiz looked at the WSKRS data coming in from the three deployed satellite probes. And he noticed something odd . . .

The temperature, the ambient water temperature, was going up . . . slowly, but crawling steadily upward.

He hit a key that would set the *seaQuest* computer to interpreting what that could mean. Perhaps there might be a need to link up with the EarthNet computer—though the ship still seemed to have a problem connecting with the UEO.

Ortiz glanced up at the station, at the spindly shapes of the smokers, the vent field behind them . . . waiting for the computer to look at the WSKRS data.

Lucas spun around in his chair.

He looked around his room, but his eyes were focused on a point miles away, thinking, wondering . . .

There's something *wrong* with the message from the UEO. Noyce had ordered the *seaQuest* into the station, but it was as if it were a one-way message, as if there were no questioning whether or not it was the right thing to do.

It felt *wrong,* thought Lucas, and he decided to look at the tape again. And again, he saw the little blips, the interruptions, the odd gestures by Noyce . . .

Did somebody have a gun to the Admiral's head, Lucas thought.

He spun around in his chair, once, then again, spinning, thinking. He looked around his room, the image of the Admiral frozen on the screen . . .

Frozen . . . captured.

Lucas stopped spinning.

He stopped and looked at the face. He let the replay run a few seconds, watched the face move, the mouth shape some words.

"Wait a second," Lucas thought.

He had an idea. He dumped about ten seconds of the video image into his computer and then started searching it with a program used for analyzing topographic maps.

"Looking for fractals," he said to himself. "Looking for little subroutines in the video image . . ."

If this were pure video feed, the program should find nothing, the image pattern would be too random, the light bouncing erratically off every surface—the Admiral's skin, his desk—impossible to reduce to a pattern.

But as soon as the program started analyzing the video dump, a green icon came on the screen—signaling that fractals, routines, had been found in the video image.

"Too . . . *much,*" Lucas said, and he hit a button and called up to the bridge.

CHAPTER 24

Rodriguez's electron-mag gun made a high-pitched squeak. A needle-thin point of light shot from the gun to a point in the center of Petersen's chest.

But Rodriguez didn't see it hit. Instead, he watched what was going on in Petersen's mouth, how the man's head seemed to twist and turn, trying to disgorge something, a blurry shape that resolved itself into one of the tube worms, wriggling out of Petersen's hideously enlarged mouth.

He heard a zap—the gun hitting. But then there was the sound of more metal gratings being kicked out, banging to the walkway.

Others were crawling out.

Still the tube worm inched its way out of Petersen, and, at the head of the creature, there were these teeth, moving, glistening.

Rodriguez fired again, but all he hit was Petersen's body, now only a dead body, slumped on the floor, while the worm pulled back and then—with terrible speed—lurched at Rodriguez.

The teeth landed on Rodriguez's chest. There was terrible pain, and then—as Rodriguez looked down, moaning—

there was nothing, just a calm peace as the creature slid its way into Rodriguez's body.

While Rodriguez let the gun fall to the walkway and waited patiently.

Terry got to the lab seconds behind Ernst and caught him opening up the refrigerated specimen cabinet.

"Put that stuff back," she said.

Ernst turned around, holding the frozen test tubes in his hands.

"You're crazy," Ernst said. "You'd let all these specimens be left here, maybe destroyed?" Ernst looked around. "This is a discovery of incredible importance. Mr. Harpe paid for it, and—"

"And you'd bring that to the surface, into the *seaQuest*? And what might happen? The same thing that happened— that's *happening*—to this station. Whatever this thing is, this worm, it can use us." Terry took a step toward Ernst. "You can't do it. Put them back. We can't—"

She heard steps. Someone following her. Probably Nathan, trying to get her to come back. He'd help her stop Ernst.

Terry turned around, but she saw a man she didn't know . . .

MacInnis looked ready to say "three." And Bridger glanced at the hatch to the shuttle. He saw a head pop up—Lieutenant Maklin—and in his hand—

"Okay," Bridger said, "Okay, everyone can come on. No problem—just let me—"

MacInnis shook his head. "No, you're trying to trick me. You're—"

Bridger caught Maklin's eyes. *No time like the present* was the message Bridger hoped he was communicating to the shuttle craft pilot.

MacInnis turned in the direction that Bridger was looking. One of the station crew said, "He's got a gun."

And Bridger watched while Maklin fired a sudden blast at MacInnis. MacInnis's eyes bulged, and then closed.

"You killed him!" someone screamed.

"No." Bridger responded. "That only knocked him out."

"And you're not going to take us!" someone else yelled.

Maklin came out of the shuttle, still holding his gun.

Bridger walked closer to the crowd. They looked so scared . . . "Now, wait a second. We *will* take you. But we aren't going to let you into the *seaQuest* until each one of you has been checked out."

There was some grumbling at this, but then they turned back to Bridger. Ready to listen.

"If you haven't been contaminated, then you'll be berthed on the *seaQuest*." Bridger paused. Here were twenty very scared people, and this could still go badly. But he saw their heads nodding. They had seen what could happen down here.

As for himself, Bridger couldn't even imagine.

"Does everyone agree?"

They nodded.

Bridger's VR-PAL radio came on again. He brought the pocket TeleCom unit up to his mouth.

"Bridger here."

He saw Ford's worried face. "Captain, is everything all right? Do you want a squad of marines sent down?"

"No, everything's fine here, Mr. Ford. We're going to bring these people up. Tell Westphalen and Shimura we want them quarantined and checked out—to make sure they haven't been in contact with the rift worms."

"Sir—we got a message. From another group of people . . ."

Bridger saw a woman move from the waiting crowd.

"That's the others," she said.

Bridger looked at her. "The others?"

She nodded. "The others . . . the ones that the worm got into, the ones it took control of . . ."

"You catching this, Lieutenant?" Bridger said.

"Yes, sir."

The woman looked away. "They got loose." She took a breath. "They're out in the station. You can't stay here. You have to leave . . ."

Bridger looked around. Where was Terry? Where was Ernst? He turned back to Maklin.

"Lieutenant, get these people on, and get ready to leave. And if I'm not back in five minutes, you leave without me."

"But Captain—"

Bridger leaned close to the sub pilot. "That's an order, Mr. Maklin. Five minutes—starting now."

Bridger ran toward the far exit, into the heart of the station.

Ortiz looked at the question posed by the analysis of the WSKRS data.

"Recommend uploading WSKRS data to LAGEOS."

Then, "Hit Y to begin upload."

LAGEOS? Why would this data about thermal variation have to be sent up to the geostationary satellite that monitored both weather and geophysical systems on the surface?

Ortiz got a funny feeling. He hit Y on his keyboard, and the data from the WSKRS probes was instantaneously zapped to the satellite.

"Transmission complete," the screen flashed.

Ortiz waited.

He glanced at Commander Ford, looking damned uncomfortable, waiting to hear from Bridger.

The screen flashed. Something was coming down from the satellite . . .

DOWNLOAD FILE RECEIVED BY SEAQUEST. Then below it, the heading FILENAME/DIRECTORY: LAGEOS/AZORES.72021.

The *seaQuest* computer automatically brought the file up.

It was brief, three pages with supporting maps and charts. Brief, and Ortiz was amazed that the information could be analyzed so quickly.

"Mr. Ford," he said quietly, "I think you should see this . . ."

Ford came over.

"WSKRS picked up—"

Ortiz flipped from the thermal gradient charts back to the LAGEOS report. Ortiz waited until Ford got down to the operative line.

"Thermal fluctuations and the location of thermal vents indicate the seafloor area is experiencing a dramatic increase in de-stability. Systems project a geophysical event of a volcanic nature within one hour."

"What?" Ford said.

"Give or take fifty minutes," Ortiz said. He spun his chair around to face the exec. "Captain Bridger's got to get out of there now. And—God, Commander Ford—we've got to get *seaQuest* out of here."

Ford turned to Bachmann. "Alert the station. Tell them to get the hell out now. And Crocker—"

The chief of the helm was waiting, his face grim. Ortiz watched Ford give the orders—and he saw how Bridger's old friend was worried.

"Set a course out of here, 155 degrees east." Away from the vent area. "Prepare to pump forward ballast."

Get the giant ship's nose up quickly.

"And set dive planes at 45 degrees."

"Whoa," Crocker said. "That's a mighty angle for the—"

Ortiz said something. "We can wait for—"

Ford turned on him. "I've sent the alert. There are nearly three hundred people on this ship. They've got ten minutes to get back, and then I'm getting the ship out of here."

Ortiz saw Crocker's face twist, as if he wanted to say something. But the chief held his tongue.

"C'mon, Captain Bridger," Ortiz said. And he wished he didn't have a digital clock in front of him.

Bridger ran full out, turning down one passageway only to realize that it led to the station crew's quarters. *The lab,* he thought, Ernst was headed toward the biology lab. And Terry was following him.

What were they walking into?

Bridger felt his heart beating, the air sucked in big gasps.

I'm out of shape, he thought. The *seaQuest* was fitted with an extensive gym, but there never seemed to be any time.

He tried to remember the research station layout as he reached the hub, the communications center. He looked back at the spoke he had come from, and tried to remember where the lab was.

Bridger counted the spokes—one . . . two . . . three . . .

He looked straight ahead. It was *that* one, and he dashed down that passageway, ignoring the burning in his lungs.

Strange . . . with each lonely, echoing step, he thought of Barbara, the dreams he had, the way he still thought of her as if she were alive. How she seemed to be asking for him to reach back in time and . . . save her.

Save her—which was something he couldn't do. He couldn't save her . . . not then, not now.

He saw doors ahead, and the sign "Deep Ocean Station Azores—Biology Laboratory."

Bridger hit a button on a wall, and the doors slid open.

Lucas grabbed Ford's arm. "Mr. Ford." The XO turned to Lucas.

"What is it, Wolenczak? We're kinda busy up here right now."

He's not crazy about me, Lucas knew. *Probably because I'm not military.* Dr. Westphalen once even described Ford as "anti-scientific."

"It wasn't Admiral Noyce," Lucas said.

"What? What are you—"

"The last transmission for the UEO. It didn't come from the UEO, and it wasn't Noyce."

Ortiz interrupted. "Mr. Ford, we're still getting an increasing temperature gradient. LAGEOS is sending out red flags all over the place."

Ford nodded at Lucas. "Wait a second." Then he turned to the communications section. "Bachmann, have you told the Captain—?"

"I've told Maklin, but the Captain isn't at the shuttle." Bachmann looked over and made an uncomfortable face. "Something's going on down there."

"Great." Then Ford turned back to Lucas. "Now, you say that it wasn't Noyce—?"

"It was a digitally constructed image, the sound was a computer construct too. Brilliant stuff—state of the art. Someone had done a sampling of Noyce and was able to build up an interactive digital picture. Best image creation I've ever seen. But it *wasn't* Noyce who told the Captain to go down to the station."

Ford pounded the arm of the empty command chair.

"Mr. Ortiz, how much time—?"

"I-I can't say. It could still be an hour, or the whole area could go volcanic in minutes."

And Ford knew that everyone on the bridge had the same horrible thought. If the area went, if a fissure opened in the ground, the *seaQuest* would most likely be trapped, destroyed.

He looked at the monitor showing the WSKRS reading of the outside water temperature. It kept going up, even well away from the smokers.

Ford came to a decision.

"Chief Crocker, power forward turbines."

The Chief looked at him.

"*Now,* Chief."

Ford walked over to Bachmann. "And keep trying to reach the Captain, for God's sake . . ."

The biology lab door slid open, and Bridger saw three people inside . . .

Ernst stood next to a large refrigerated specimen cabinet. His hand was on the door, and he held test tubes in the other. And opposite, there was a man, someone Bridger didn't know, someone from the research station standing with his back to Bridger.

Terry was across the room, backed against the wall, her face twisted, her eyes wide—

Bridger said, "Let's go—back to the shuttle. And no samples, Dr. Ernst—"

Terry shook her head . . . and spoke.

"Nathan—get—"

The man with his back to Bridger turned around. Bridger saw his name patch. Rodriguez. He was smiling. Bridger smiled back—

Until he saw the hole in the man's chest. A great bloody cannonball-sized opening . . . with something below the surface, moving . . . alive.

There was no way the man could be alive, not with a wound of that size—and yet he was.

Rodriguez nodded. "Yes, let's all go to the shuttle." He turned to Terry, then back to Ernst. "That's a good idea."

Bridger backed up.

Thinking: *I don't even have a gun. What the hell is wrong with me? No weapon—*

Though he didn't know what was going on with Rodriguez, he knew that a gun would have made him feel a *lot* better.

Bridger looked at Terry, and—by making his eyes dart back and forth—he tried signaling that he wanted her to move closer to him. Terry took one step, and then another.

Rodriguez turned and looked at her. "Where are you going? What are you—?"

The thing in the hole, in Rodriguez's wound, came closer to the surface, and Bridger saw the whitish skin, and an opening, a mouth of some kind.

This is one for the movies, Bridger thought. *If I was filming this, no one would believe it.*

Terry stopped moving.

The thing in the hole edged out a bit more.

Bridger thought, *Something bad is going to happen. Unless I do something, something very bad is going to happen . . .*

Which was when Dr. Richard Ernst made his move.

Westphalen was on the bridge, standing next to Ortiz and Ford, looking at the wide view of the hydrothermal field.

"Do you agree?" Ford said.

Westphalen nodded, almost reluctantly.

"Look," she explained, "the flow of hydrogen sulfites has increased. Something's happening, a change in the geology of the area—that's certain."

Ford took a breath. "Then we have to leave."

Westphalen looked at him. "But what about the Captain?"

Ford looked at the screen, and then the vent area that was expected to blow—anytime now.

"I hope he gets out."

Ernst looked left and right. There was another door leading off the lab. Bridger watched the scientist look at it, hesitating, thinking . . . and then—steeling himself for a dash.

Ernst ran to the door.

What happened next was so brutally fast that Bridger held his breath.

Ernst ran four, five steps, until he was only a foot away from this other door leading off the lab.

And—without Rodriguez moving—the worm shot out of his chest, a long ribbony line suddenly stretching all the way to Ernst.

It hit him in the side just as his hand was reaching out for the handle. Then, as if Ernst were feeling some kind of back pain, he reached behind him . . .

There were sounds—the sound of skin tearing, the small yelps that Ernst made. Horrible sounds.

For the worm, it was an opportunity.

"Terry," Bridger yelled, and she ran over to him as he hit the button opening the lab door. The doors seemed to take forever, and he saw Rodriguez or whatever this thing was now, turning to him even as it dragged Ernst toward itself.

Come on . . . , Bridger begged as the door seemed to take forever to slide open.

Come—

The door was open, but as Bridger pushed Terry through, he looked over his shoulder and saw the worm—completely imbedded in Ernst now, the two figures joined together—split with a loud *snap.*

Then there were two of them, pulling back, ready to leap at Terry and him.

He hit the button on the other side, and the door started to slide shut—

The worms landed at the closing door with a greasy *splat*.

Bridger started running, pulling Terry. He had told Maklin to wait five minutes. How much time had passed?

Three, four minutes.

"There must"—Terry's voice gasped from the effort of the full-out run—"be . . . more."

"What?" Bridger said.

They turned the corner.

"Prepare to take her up . . . Dive planes set, Mr. Crocker? Engine one-quarter. Trim aft ballast."

"Damn," Crocker said.

But Ford didn't let the Chief's complaint pass unnoticed. "I gave an order, Mr. Crocker. An order to save this ship. And I expect it to be obeyed."

He turned to Bachmann. "What's the shuttle doing, Mr. Bachmann?"

"Maklin is still alone. He's loaded the station crew into the shuttle. They'll have to be quarantined. I've already alerted Dr. Shimura."

"And Bridger?"

Bachmann looked sick. "No word, Mr. Ford."

People stood in the passageway.

But even in the faint light Bridger saw that they had wounds of some kind.

"No good," Bridger said.

Terry looked around. "We can get to one of the other modules off the station by going down one of these passageways."

There were passageways left and right. And surely they would lead them *somewhere*—unless they led to a locked module—and then they'd have to snake their way to the sub bay.

Bridger looked behind him, and he saw two other figures coming toward them—

One of them looked like Ernst.

"Which way?" Bridger said. And Terry looked left and then right, and then—as if it were only a guess—she tore off down the right passageway.

As they ran, Bridger thought that there could be even more of them ahead, more of these people who weren't people anymore, their bodies hosts to something so strange, so alien, it belonged on another planet.

He had to wonder: What kept these incredibly opportunistic creatures trapped here? What had kept them imprisoned until now?

They reached another module, and looking at Terry, Bridger knew that she heard what he heard—the sound of feet behind them.

"The sub pool is down that way," she said.

"*If* there's time," he added.

Maklin had the station crew loaded on the shuttle—except for one man who stood on the dock.

"Sir, you'd better get in."

The man nodded. "Why, yes, I suppose that's a good idea."

Captain Bridger had ordered Maklin to leave—after five minutes. And that time was almost up.

The man looked at Maklin. "You're not actually going to leave?"

Maklin looked around. He knew that the *seaQuest* was preparing to leave the area; he knew that what was happening inside the station was *nothing* compared to what might happen outside it if the vent area went.

"I was ordered to—"

Then the side doors leading to the small sub pool kicked open. The two of them turned around to see . . .

Captain Bridger running in.

"Mr. Ford!" Bachmann yelled. "The Captain's back, he's getting the shuttle under way . . ."

Ford looked at Crocker. "Hold our position, Chief. Keep me posted on their progress, Bachmann . . . and tell them to get a move on."

Bridger hopped onto the metal dock next to the shuttle, followed by Terry McShane.

"I told you to leave, Lieutenant."

"Sir, I—"

Bridger smiled. "Forget it. You're all loaded? And *seaQuest* is ready for the quarantine?"

Wouldn't it be fun if one of these people had a worm inside them . . . and we brought it on board, Bridger thought.

"Sir—she's standing by, but she's about to leave the area."

Bridger looked at Terry, then at the man on the dock . . . looking down at the door.

"Leave the area? What's the—"

"Sir, the vent area is unstable. There are reports of geologic activity of some kind."

"Great. Well, let's get—"

But the doors down at the far end opened, and then the people streamed in, the people with the wounds, like wounded shoppers at a white sale, bursting through the doors, each one carrying the telltale sign of something wrong—a big bloody gouge here, an opening in a stomach there. A few were linked, two people now one creature.

"Get in!" Bridger yelled.

Then the man next to Bridger held up his gun.

"No—you get in, Captain. If they keep coming, your sub won't get out of here."

"You'll be killed—"

"Captain . . . please, allow me one moment of bravery in my life."

Bridger hesitated, and then got in behind Maklin and Terry.

"Now shut the hatch!"

"Shut the hatch," Dell said.

So out of character for me, he thought, *to play the hero.*

Not exactly a role I was auditioning for. Still, there was something to be said for this moment of glory.

He heard the shuttle hatch lock, the engines whirring.

Dell took a step off the metal dock.

"Okay, keep coming," he said, looking at the advancing crowd.

He raised the electron-mag gun. It was set to kill, naturally, though he doubted it would.

And, as he had suspected, the creatures looked at the sub, realizing that their only link to the outside world was leaving.

One of the worms began to slither out.

How strong was it? thought Dell. Could it grab onto the side of the sub, grab on, hold on—

All the way into *seaQuest*?

Dell fired. The worm recoiled. Another worm shot out, trying to reach the water of the sub bay, and Dell fired again.

Though the gun was set to kill, the worm still *moved.*

No matter—they still recoiled, and Dell walked toward them, firing, aiming at the masters inside the human hosts . . . while the shuttle disappeared from the pool.

Bridger saw Ford's face on the screen, and he looked mighty relieved.

"Mr. Ford, I'm not sure you should have waited. We could have rendezvoused near the surface . . ."

Ford smiled. "I was just about to leave, Captain."

From the porthole, Bridger saw the station behind him as the shuttle streamed away from the vent area.

Everything was going to turn out all right, he thought. Hard to believe but—

There was a rumble. Maklin looked at Bridger, a sick expression on his face. Then Bridger turned back to Ford on the screen. His face showed no recognition. It was too small a rumble for Ford to hear. But then—

Ford turned away. "Mr. Ortiz tells me that there's been some activity, Captain."

"I know," Bridger said.

Bridger looked back at the Azores station personnel . . . A few minutes ago they had been relieved to be safe, and now—

There was another shock, then another—

The shuttle craft rocked left, and then right.

"Keep her steady, Lieutenant Maklin," Bridger said. "Hold onto the stick."

Then there was a big boom, and an underwater shock wave hit the shuttle, threatening to turn the sub upside down.

The image of Ford on the screen broke up and then reappeared.

"Take *seaQuest* out of here, Mr. Ford," Bridger said.

Bridger knew that Ford was dealing with the information pouring into the bridge. He looked back at the camera lens. "What's that, Captain? I'm having trouble understanding you."

Sure you are, Bridger thought.

"Captain," Maklin said. "Another blast like that and we're in trouble. The shuttle's not designed to withstand blows like that."

"Show me the vent field," Bridger said.

The screen displayed the view from the rear.

The field was dark, the station lights looking like small stars in the night-colored sea. But then there were small glowing plumes erupting from the tops of the chimneys, glowing, growing bigger.

First one, then another, until it was like a torchlight ceremony.

Bridger, who had studied such phenomena at Scripps Oceanographic, knew what to expect.

Terry, sitting right behind him, grabbed his arm.

"Are we going to make it?"

He turned to her and whispered, "Can you count to ten?"

She licked her lips. She mouthed the word. *One* . . .

The glowing plumes atop the smokers grew larger, until, like molten ice cream, the yellow lava dripped down the sides.

There was another shock wave, as a pair of chimneys had exploded, leaving an open hole, a glowing wound, spreading.

The seafloor was cracking, the lava building until—Bridger was sure—a major sea quake would turn the entire vent field into a fiery hell.

He looked at Terry. *Four. Five. Six.*

Seven.

"How far is *seaQuest*?" Bridger asked.

Maklin was struggling to remain calm. "Almost there," Maklin said. "We're almost—"

"Let me see her."

There on the screen, so close, was the ship, looking like a sleeping phosphorescent creature of the deep.

My ship, thought Bridger . . . wondering if he'd ever be inside it again.

Another shock wave rattled the shuttle.

The people behind him remained stoically calm. They had been through a lot, and were still hanging in there.

After an eternity, Maklin said—

"Ready to enter *seaQuest*, sir."

"All set, Lieutenant," Ford said.

The shuttle headed for the brightly lit opening leading to the ship's mammoth moon pool. The *seaQuest* grew on the VR screen, until the well-lit entranceway filled it. Bridger held his breath, as he was sure everyone else did.

Terry whispered the word "Ten . . ."

And they were *in.*

Bridger wasted no time, even as the shuttle started to surface in the pool.

"Get us out of here, Mr. Ford."

The shuttle bobbed to the surface, and Maklin hit a button releasing the hatch. And as soon as the hatch was open, Bridger saw Shimura and three guards waiting on the dock, holding onto the railing as each shock wave rattled the ship.

There was a flash of silver, and Darwin leapt into the air.

Bridger smiled.

"Good to see you, Dar."

"Good to see *you*," Darwin said. Then, with Terry by his side, Bridger started for his bridge, to take command. The dolphin spoke, the voice clear through the speakers in the pool.

"Danger not . . . over."

They watched the end via the WSKRS.

Telephoto lenses scanned the vent area and yet kept the probes a reasonably safe distance away.

The entire vent area was now a burning yellow-gold mass laced with ribbons of red. The temperature in spots passed the thousand-degree mark.

The station had been slowly covered with a coating of the molten flow, now dripping down the natural slope of the vent area.

That ended it, thought Bridger. It *was* all over—the strange worms, the discovery of these chemosynthesizers who seemed to have their hungry eye on the rest of the planet.

Terry sipped a cup of tea. There was plenty of work to be done—files to be analyzed, contact with Noyce, discovering who had sent the phony transmission—Lucas was so excited about his discovery.

But for now they all watched the death of the vent area with an odd sort of reverence. The area seemed to flicker, and then explode, sending rock and lava flying up as the seafloor remade itself . . .

And the crew on the bridge of the *seaQuest* had to look away from the brilliant glow on the VR screens.

EPILOGUE

After getting a night's restless sleep that turned into an
unseemly twelve hours, Bridger got up and checked in with
his crew chiefs.

He started with the medical center of the *seaQuest*.

Shimura rubbed the skin on his arm while talking to
Bridger. "They all check out, Captain. No sign of any
unusual cell formations, viral or otherwise, in any of the
station crew. In my opinion, you can take the station people off quarantine."

The *seaQuest* was headed to the Flamingo port in southern Florida. The Azores station people were to be off-loaded
to a medical facility there and—Bridger had heard—Terry
McShane would be getting off as well.

Bridger had hoped that she'd go on to San Francisco with
seaQuest, that there would be some time there for them to
talk, to see whether there was any future for the two of them.

"Let's keep an eye on them anyway, Akira."

Shimura touched Bridger's arm. "Trust me, they're okay.
But, Nathan, I think you'd better check Darwin."

"There's something wrong with Dar's communication
rig?"

Shimura smiled. "No, Darwin is fine, the rig is working okay. But—just make sure you talk to Darwin soon . . . about what happened."

"Will do—"

Bill Noyce clicked off the screen in his office. It had been impossible to trace the signal, to find out who had tampered with the UEO's message.

But I sure as hell can guess who did it, Noyce thought.

No question about it. And it could have been a major disaster—instead of—

Noyce smiled . . .

Merely losing a billion-plus project and sixteen lives.

Geoffrey Harpe would have to be watched. The UEO's board would have to take him as a threat, someone who was willing to use disaster if there was profit to be made.

Later—there would have to be an accounting with Nathan Hale Bridger. Would Bridger quit over this? After all, he hadn't been told the truth. *He'll never trust me again,* Noyce thought.

That was too bad.

And a gallon of ice cream wouldn't make amends this time.

The Flamingo Sub Station was a commercial venture. But security was provided by the UEO, and the arrival of *seaQuest* was an event.

Bridger came down from the bridge to find Terry sitting in her cabin, her bag packed.

"It's been an eventful couple of weeks for you, Terry."

She looked up, her face stolid, and Bridger wondered whether he was crazy to think that there were possibilities here, that he could reach out for someone again.

She nodded.

He said, "No way you could continue to San Francisco?"

"No, Nate. There will be special hearings about both incidents in New York. I'll be tied up in multinational court stuff for months." Her smile broadened. "My days of adventuring are over for a while."

Bridger came close. His hand reached out, tentative, almost embarrassed. He brushed her hair. "A good thing too."

Her hand reached up for his . . . and she stood up.

Bridger looked away, the eye contact too intense. *God, he thought, I'm so out of practice with all this . . . It's like learning how to date all over again.*

"Terry, I don't—"

She took the lead, pulling him close. "So—you go to San Francisco, Nathan, and I go to New York. But surely you'll bring your ship east again. The *Intrepid*'s looking a little sad on Forty-sixth Street. How about it . . . ?"

His eyes turned to hers again—and they kissed, Bridger holding her tight, wishing that they were on his island together, and the afternoon could simply melt into night.

But then they were interrupted by a voice announcing that the Flamingo port was dead ahead—and for now, it all came to a stop.

Terry didn't look back when she climbed the steps to the shuttle to take her to the surface. When she got out, Flamingo Harbor would be filled with curious vacationers eager for a chance to see the minisub from one of the world's wonders, *seaQuest DSV*.

The Azores station crew had already left in another shuttle, and was quickly loaded into buses from the Miami Medical Center.

Bridger watched Terry as she left.

He wondered—*Does she feel as bad as I do? I thought I could lose myself in the work here, on the sub. But—maybe—it's not enough.*

Just as she was nearly inside, Terry turned and waved.

Bridger smiled and nodded. Then Terry McShane vanished into the shuttle and the hatch closed.

He watched the shuttle disappear under the water, leaving *seaQuest*.

"Darwin's looking good, eh, Captain?"

Katherine Hitchcock stood next to the large tank on the bridge.

Bridger remembered what Shimura had said.

But Darwin looked fine. His eyes were clear, and despite the wound behind his head, the dolphin moved smoothly back and forth inside the tank.

"You look great, Darwin. How do you feel?"

"I . . . feel good."

Bridger studied the dolphin for any sign that something was wrong, but Darwin seemed okay.

There were a lot of things to be checked before setting off down to the Canal—and San Francisco . . . and a confrontation with Bill Noyce.

"That's great." Bridger smiled at Hitchcock, and walked away.

But Darwin followed, and the speaker above the tank crackled.

"Captain . . ."

Bridger stopped. It always felt odd to hear the dolphin address him as "Captain."

"Yes, Dar—"

"Captain, there are more . . ."

Bridger looked at Darwin. "More? What do you mean, Darwin. More of what . . . ?"

The dolphin swam a lazy O in the tank.

Bridger looked at Hitchcock, but the chief engineer shook her head. She didn't know what the dolphin was referring to . . .

"More places . . . more worms. There are *more* of them."

Bridger stopped. How could Darwin know that? Sure, he was linked to the computer system. But Westphalen had only guessed that there were more of them—and now Darwin was—what?

Warning him . . .

He felt Hitchcock watching to see if there was any reaction.

Bridger nodded.

Later, he'd have to talk to Darwin in detail. Was it possible that the creature could not only communicate, but also have hunches . . . intuition . . . or maybe something more?

I'll believe anything, Bridger thought.

"That may be, Darwin. And if there are, we'll find them."

He reached up and rapped the tank, a bit of old-fashioned communication, and then he turned back to the fore section of the bridge . . . where his crew waited.

Rafael was shadowing the scruffy deep-sea mining transport working the Santos Plateau, off Brazil.

Perhaps the transport has picked us up, he thought . . . Perhaps . . . But it wouldn't matter. After all, what could they do?

There were maybe fifty . . . maybe seventy-five people on board. And they had miles to go to get back to their station.

"I don't understand, Rafael. Why are we doing this?"

Rafael turned from the screen that tracked the transport. Ozawa, his first mate, stood next to the team who manned the sub's command center.

"I-I don't see the reason. A mining transport, it doesn't make sense."

But Rafael smiled. "Oh, but it will make sense, Ozawa. First we attack this mining transport, then the mining colony itself, and then a deep-sea farming commune, and eventually, they will have to send her . . ."

Martin stood there, waiting.

"They will have to send *seaQuest,* and send Nathan Hale Bridger . . . and when that happens, we will be ready for her, to destroy that great ship."

Ozawa nodded, but Rafael knew that his friend didn't share his commitment to this concept, this idea of revenge. That might be a problem that would have to be dealt with.

Rafael turned back to the transport.

"Targeting display!" Rafael said, and immediately a screen showed a circular matrix with an icon of the transport at the center.

"Display up," Martin said.

"Flood forward tubes one through four," Rafael said, savoring the moment, the transport so much like a stupid, innocent rabbit about to get its head blown off.

Ozawa answered, "Tubes flooded."

"Arm e-plasma torpedoes."

"Torpedoes armed. Rafael, don't you think we should be planning—"

Rafael turned to his number two. "No, I don't. And don't you dare test my friendship, my loyalty, by questioning another one of my commands."

He turned back to the targeting display. "Fire forward torpedoes."

The targeting display changed to a live image of the transport making its slow way over a rocky seafloor, heading home.

Even now, thought Rafael, they were picking up the warning, the alarm that the torpedoes were heading toward them.

"Three . . . two . . ."

Rafael licked his lips.

Then—there was a brilliant explosion that filled the screen with a yellow-white phosphorescence.

When the picture cleared, there was nothing there.

The transport had been reduced to so much garbage.

And, thought Rafael, a chill would settle over the deep-sea communities in this part of the Atlantic. There was a wolf there, a raider.

After enough raids, the *seaQuest* would come.

And I will wait for her, thought Rafael . . .

"Captain, the shuttle has returned, and *seaQuest* is secured and ready to leave Flamingo Harbor, sir."

Bridger smiled at Ford. "Mr. Ford, I didn't get to tell you what fine work you did back there. You thought of *seaQuest* first, her crew, and took quick action. It was good work . . ."

Ford smiled back. "But sir . . . weren't you upset that a few minutes more and we would have left you behind?"

"Oh, on a personal level I might have been a tad disappointed." Bridger grinned. "But it was a good decision." Bridger sat in the command chair.

"Captain, the harbor authority has cleared *seaQuest* for departure."

"Next time, though, I think you can be the one to play

'beat the clock.' " Ford laughed. "I'm getting too old for this stuff . . ."

They both laughed, and Bridger felt that—for the first time—he was starting to bond with his exec. There was still quite a way to go, in terms of trust and friendship, but this had been a start.

"Plot a course, Mr. Ford. The Panama Canal, if you remember."

"Aye, aye, sir," Ford said.

Crocker looked back to Bridger. "Will we be taking her farther down, sir?"

"Not yet, Gator."

On the VR screen, Bridger looked at the blue water of the harbor, lit by the bright morning sunshine.

"There's plenty of deep-ocean time to come."

"Course plotted, Captain."

"Good, Mr. Ford. Set that course, stabilize ballast and—since we're late for our conference, gentlemen—full speed ahead . . ."

Captain Nathan Hale Bridger sat back in his command chair, thinking of Terry but also enjoying the feeling of commanding this ship, this *seaQuest,* as it sailed under the choppy water of the Gulf of Mexico.